SECRET SANTA

Also by Andrew Shaffer

Obama Biden Mysteries

Hope Rides Again

Hope Never Dies

Parodies and Satires

The Day of the Donald: Trump Trumps America!

Ghosts from Our Past: Both Literally and Figuratively: The Study of the Paranormal

Catsby: A Parody

How to Survive a Sharknado and Other Unnatural Disasters

Fifty Shames of Earl Grey: A Parody

Nonfiction

Literary Rogues: A Scandalous History of Wayward Authors

Great Philosophers Who Failed at Love

SECRET SANTA

ANDREW SHAFFER

QUIRK BOOKS
PHILADELPHIA

Dedicated to the memory of my middle school English teacher, Kate "Kathleen" Finn, who told me I could be the next Stephen King if I kept writing. Alas, there's only one King of Horror, but her encouragement was one of the cornerstones to finding my own voice.

Library of Congress Cataloging in Publication Data
Shaffer, Andrew, author.
Secret Santa / Andrew Shaffer.
Summary: "As soon as Lussi Meyer arrives at the prestigious Blackwood-Patterson publishing house, she finds herself the target of mean-spirited pranks by her coworkers. After receiving a strange present during the company's annual Secret Santa gift exchange, her coworkers begin falling victim to horrific accidents, and Lussi suspects her gift may be involved"—Provided by publisher.
LCSH: Christmas stories. | Paranormal fiction. | GSAFD: Black humor (Literature) | Horror fiction. | LCGFT: Novels.
LCC PS3613.E7566 S43 2020 | DDC 813/.6—dc23   2020038776

ISBN: 978-1-68369-205-8

Printed in the United States of America

Typeset in Bembo and Albertus

Designed by Ryan Hayes
Cover illustration by Adam Rabalais
Production management by John J. McGurk

Quirk Books
215 Church Street
Philadelphia, PA 19106
quirkbooks.com

10 9 8 7 6 5 4 3 2 1

"A gift isn't a gift unless it has meaning."
—Oprah Winfrey

"What's in the box?"
—Brad Pitt, *Se7en*

PROLOGUE

The war was over. Millions of Allied troops had already returned home. In a few hours they would begin waking up to the sound of delighted squeals as Santa's bounty was discovered under the tree. They might turn over, notice the indent in their wife's mattress. Hear the coffee machine percolating—not Army mud, but real, fresh-ground beans. Smell the sweet aroma of sizzling bacon strips. Wonder what in God's name they'd done to get so lucky.

Xavier Blackwood, MP with the Army's 3rd Infantry Division, wasn't lucky. Some fathead in the War Department had concocted a point system for demobilization. It was complicated, but favored those with children. Those with families of their own. For Xavier, who hadn't had the foresight to knock some rusty hen up before being shipped out, the war continued.

"So this is Christmas," he said, slipping a cigarette from his deck. With the blustering wind, it took him three tries to light it. He passed the lighter to Duluth, a fellow MP on the night shift. The two of them were deep in the woods behind the barracks; a light snow was falling. They'd abandoned their posts at 0500 hours, telling no one where they were going. Secrecy was of the utmost importance. Not even their superiors had been briefed. Xavier and Duluth had concocted the mission themselves, after many hours of passing a bottle of Hennessy cognac back and forth: they were going to surprise the boys back at base with a real live Christmas tree.

"You hear about Manila?" Duluth said, trudging through the snow.

Xavier nodded. Thousands of disgruntled soldiers had staged a protest over the bungled demobilization strategy. At least, that was the rumor. Sounded a lot like mutiny to Xavier. Whatever you called it, the natives were getting restless.

"You're a three-year man like me, right?" the kid continued.

"Come April," Xavier said.

"Same. We should be able to get the hell out of here by then. My girl said she would keep the tree up in our apartment until I got back. Told her the only present I wanted was her under it, wearing nothing but a bow."

Xavier blew out a smoke ring. He hadn't been a smoker prior to the war. "She won't last that long."

"The tree? Sure she will. It's one of those new, whaddaya-call-it, artificial trees."

"I was talking about your girl," Xavier said.

The kid spun on him, throwing an elbow into his gut. The fireman's axe slipped from Xavier's fingers into the snow. He doubled over to catch his breath. When he righted himself, he leaned on the trunk of a barren oak.

The kid was laughing now, bent over. Tears streaming down his face.

Xavier picked up the axe, dusted the snow off it. "The hell's so funny?"

"I don't have a girl back home," Duluth said. "I had one, but she stopped writing me." He stood up straight. "Hit me. Then we'll be hunky-dory. Not with the axe, though—I want to get out of this godforsaken country, but not that bad."

"Listen to you, wanting to be the next Houdini."

The kid looked at him blankly.

"Before your time, I guess," Xavier said. Duluth was an infantry-man from Minnesota who had joined them at Merkers. "Duluth" was his hometown; Xavier had forgotten the kid's Christian name. Said he was twenty-one in ten days, but he didn't look old enough to drive. Xavier would be thirty this year. In the war, however, age wasn't important. All that mattered was time served. In that respect, they were equals.

Xavier handed him the fire axe. "I'll let you do the chopping when we find—"

"What about this one?" Duluth said, pointing the axe at an evergreen that stretched to the heavens.

Xavier weighed their options. They'd been walking through the woods for almost an hour. Searching for the right-sized tree. Maybe there was no right-sized tree. The sun would be up soon. The morning crew would be coming around to relieve them and notice them missing. Xavier didn't want to wind up on spud duty again.

"Show me what you got, kid."

Duluth lined up his shot at the base and swung. The fire axe flew from his hand like a shot put, sailing past the tree and landing in a dense thatch of twigs, where the snow erupted into a small mushroom cloud. Duluth dropped to his knees and began pound-ing the tree with closed fists.

Xavier stared on, stone-faced. Perhaps he should have slugged the punk when he had the chance. Knock some sense into him. He lowered his head and started for the axe. Xavier was sobering up now. Fast. The stupidity of their "mission" was only now hitting him. What were they going to decorate the tree with, anyway? They had no ornaments, no tinsel. No lights. No gifts to stack underneath.

He saw the glimmer of metal in the snow and bent to pick it up. Only it wasn't the axe.

Xavier's breath hitched. Maybe his eyes were playing tricks on him, but the half-buried object glittering in the moonlight looked an awful lot like the rounded edge of a land mine. He didn't have any interest in dusting the snow off and investigating. Before the war, he'd just been a gangly fellow working behind the circulation desk of the Brooklyn branch of the New York Public Library. He wanted to return, long limbs and all.

"Hurry up, I'm freezing out here," Duluth said, stumbling toward him. "My wool underwear is starting to itch. At least I hope it's my underwear that's itching."

Xavier turned in time to see the kid trip on a fallen trunk and hurtle toward him. There was no time to scream. They tumbled backward in a heap, landing squarely on whatever was buried in the snow. For a split second—a split second was long enough, though—Xavier felt the rounded metal edge digging into his lower back.

He threw Duluth off him and rolled to the side in one fluid motion, holding onto his helmet in hopes it would protect his brain from the worst of the shrapnel.

Seconds passed. Xavier heard the kid laughing. Xavier rolled up to a sitting position, head and limbs intact. The axe lay next to him. He could see now that what they'd rolled over wasn't a land mine, but the steel-toed sole of a boot. A body, buried in a winter wonderland.

Xavier hurriedly shoveled snow away from the frozen figure. A Luger pistol shone in the half-moon next to the rigid body. If there'd been any question, the red armband around the upper right arm confirmed it.

"A dead rat," Duluth said, his voice a hoarse whisper.

Xavier brushed the snow away from the corpse's face to get a look at the man. Only there was no face. Just a black hole. Xavier shined the right-angle head of his flashlight on the caved-in skull. Teeth and red bits of muscle spilled from the hole like guts of a jack-o-lantern left on the porch too long.

Xavier heard the kid vomit. It smelled of cognac and corned-beef hash.

The dead body had no smell.

"Where's his face?" Duluth said. "Something ate his face."

Xavier shook his head. "He killed himself. I've seen this type of injury before. Muzzle in the mouth, pointed upward. Blew the front of his face off."

"Jesus."

"He was lucky," Xavier said. "Sometimes they live."

The dead man had clearly come out here with one purpose in mind. You didn't get dressed up in your SS best just to go for a holiday stroll through the woods. Something else struck Xavier as odd. He had no idea how long the body had been out here, but scavengers should have come by now. Vultures. Wolves. It was like they could smell the evil on this man, the poison in his veins. Nazis were so foul that not even flies would lay eggs in their corpses.

Duluth kicked at a wooden box next to the man. "What is this? A Christmas present?" he said. The box was rectangular, about half the size of a rucksack. An iron padlock held the clasp together.

Xavier gripped the axe. "Step aside."

Duluth moved away from the box. Xavier brought the axe down on the lock once, twice. On the third try, the iron split apart. He crouched and tossed the pieces aside. The lid lifted with ease. Xavier shined his flashlight into the box . . . and, though he didn't yet know what he was looking at, he knew at once what it could do.

Xavier felt something wash over him.

Warm.

Dark.

Terrifying.

Thrilling.

He wanted to hold on to the feeling forever.

Duluth asked what was in the box. "Nazi gold? Please tell me it's Nazi gold. I could use some spending money."

Xavier backed away to let the kid have a look.

"What . . . that's it?" Duluth said, his voice full of disappointment.

Xavier dropped the flashlight into the snow. The beam angled up, its light going on and off at intervals like orange bursts from a machine gun at night. "Your batteries die?" Duluth asked. "I think I've got some spares . . ." The kid's voice trailed off as he slowly raised his eyes to meet Xavier's. "Everything okay, man? You don't look so good."

Xavier Blackwood, MP with the Army's 3rd Infantry Division, raised the axe high overhead. "Everything's . . . hunky-dory," he said in the flickering light.

CHAPTER ONE

New York City
December 1, 1986

Lussi walked up to the front of the Blackwood Building on Avenue A. Although she'd heard the publisher's East Village headquarters was unusual, she wasn't prepared for it to be *this* unusual. The four-story brownstone was black. Solid black. At first she thought it was a paint job to make it look sleek and modern, but as she lowered her sunglasses she could see that any appearance of modernity was an illusion. The sandstone was blackened with soot and city grime, the result of decades of neglect. Even more unusual were the wrought-iron bars on the windows—not just the street-level windows, but all four stories. Was this a publishing house or a Victorian insane asylum? Needless to say, it was love at first sight.

"Move it or lose it, yuppie scum," a geriatric bag lady said, emerging from the shadows of the alley wheeling a cart full of empty liquor bottles.

"Did you call me a yuppie?" Lussi said, clutching her Coach purse under her armpit and stepping out of the woman's way. The name-brand purse wasn't even hers; she'd borrowed it from her roommate. Lussi noticed more down-on-their-luck sorts across the street. So this was Tompkins Square Park. She'd read in the papers that it had been taken over by a homeless camp, which she could now see for herself. Amidst the tents and tarps, rough-looking men were huddled around burning barrels. A tall, thin man in a fedora from some bygone era was standing beyond the barrels. Through the smoke, he seemed to be studying her with intense curiosity.

Lussi turned sharply back to the building. She took a deep breath and smoothed her houndstooth print skirt. Her best stir-rup pants were tucked into her polished Mary Janes. She checked her makeup in her compact. *Maybe I am yuppie scum*, she thought, smoothing her ponytail in its black velvet scrunchie.

She marched up the imposing stone steps and hit the buzzer.

"Name," a voice full of static demanded.

"Lussi Meyer," she said.

"Do you have an appointment?"

"An interview. My name sounds like 'Lucy,' but it's spelled L-U-S—"

There was a whir, followed by a clank. She tried the door, but it didn't budge.

"Wait for the rest, please," the voice said.

Lussi stepped back as the whirring and clanking continued. She counted six locks before the iron door finally creaked open an inch. It was so heavy, she had to wedge her shoulder against it and push. It almost felt like the door was pushing back, like it didn't want to let her in. Eventually, it gave in and swung open, sending Lussi stumbling into the cavernous lobby. She came to a stop a foot from bowling over a decorated Christmas tree. A trim reception-ist, seated behind a wide desk, raised a sculpted eyebrow. Above, on the third-floor landing, an elegant woman with a fashionable bottle-blond buzz cut sipped from a highball glass, eyes on Lussi.

Lussi approached the front desk. "I have an eleven thirty with Mr. Blackwood."

The receptionist put a hand over her headset's mouthpiece and pointed to the stairs. "Fourth floor. Oh, and I love your purse."

"Thank you," she said, mounting the winding staircase strung with white Christmas lights. "I love yours . . . too . . ."

Lussi's voice trailed off as she found herself mesmerized not by the woman's purse—there wasn't one on her desk—but by the interior of the building. It was all tarnished brass and chipped marble, carved wood accents and warm lighting. So different from the harsh fluorescents and bare drywall at her last job.

She paused on the third-floor landing to listen to the click-clacking chorus of typewriters from deep within the building. None of those electric gizmos, either. Heavy, manual typewriters that sounded like her mother's. Lussi scanned the postings on a rectangular corkboard, hoping to gain some insight into the company culture. Amidst workplace safety regulations and minimum-wage posters was a handwritten memo about the company-wide Secret Santa gift exchange, scheduled for December 12. *Leave your presents under the tree anytime between now and then, but remember!! It's supposed to be anonymous, so leave YOUR name off!!*

Could this place be any quainter?

The double doors at the top of the stairs opened into a waiting area staffed by a blue-haired woman older than Cthulhu. The fourth floor was even more resplendent than the entryway, if such a thing were possible. The floor-to-ceiling windows were draped with heavy red velvet curtains, which looked like they'd been stripped from a Hammer film set. The wood-paneled walls were lined with built-in bookcases. She imagined she was looking at first editions of every novel Blackwood-Patterson had published since its inception in 1947. The room smelled like dried glue and dusty paper . . . the smell of old books. The smell of happiness.

Blackwood-Patterson hadn't been on her short list of places

to work. It hadn't even been on her long list. But this . . . this was beyond all expectations. She was going to cry if she didn't get this job. This was as old-school publishing as you could get, a holdover from an era she'd only heard tall tales of. The skyscrapers of Midtown had nothing on the Blackwood Building. If the employees were even half as charming, this was a place she could see herself working for a long, long time.

CHAPTER TWO

When Lussi was shown into Mr. Blackwood's office, she found him seated behind a green leather-topped mahogany desk, his white hair in a perfect widow's peak. If his secretary was ancient, then he was positively prehistoric. Mr. Blackwood made no move to rise. Instead, he motioned for her to take a seat across from him.

"Miss Meyer." His voice was cool yet polite.

The enormous club chair made her feel smaller than her five-foot-two frame. As she struggled to get comfortable, he stared at her over long, steepled fingers.

"This won't take long," he said. "I can already tell you won't do."

She stopped fussing around. "I'm sorry, I think I misheard you."

He held up a sheaf of paper, which trembled in his liver-spotted hand. "I've interviewed all ten of you to make Agnes happy. But I'm afraid I've already chosen our new editor. He's very qualified. A Skull and Bones man, like myself. No need to prolong the inevitable. You may go."

Lussi was dumbstruck. She couldn't believe it. She refused to. She hadn't spent the last of her checking account to get her bangs professionally trimmed and feathered only to be kicked to the curb after half a minute.

"Mr. Blackwood, forgive me, but you're making a big mistake." His eyebrows shot up. Encouraged by his shock, she continued. "When was the last time a Blackwood-Patterson book hit the *Times* list?"

"I have the feeling you're about to tell me."

"August 1984. Over two years ago. And that was only for one week before dropping off. Before that, another two years. Now, I don't know about my competition, but during the past five years at Broken Angel, I've had thirteen *New York Times* best sellers."

He sighed heavily and held out his hand. "Your resume, please?"

She whisked another copy out of her purse. Good thing she'd run off enough to paper the town.

He perused it with a blank face. "Let's take a look at your work . . . *The Kitchen Demon*? A marital drama, I assume."

It was a novel about a possessed kitchen mixer.

"Something like that," she said. "It debuted at number eight on the paperback list and hung on for three months."

"Paperbacks," he muttered, as if it were a swear word. "We're in the hardcovers business here. Who is this . . . Nightingale? Fabien Nightingale? That's not the gentleman with the long hair on the bodice rippers, is it?"

She almost laughed—the thought of Fabien on the cover of a romance novel was too much. He wrote like Edgar Allan Poe, dressed like Oscar Wilde, and drank like William Faulkner. "I believe you're thinking of Fabio."

Mr. Blackwood rolled his eyes. "And this Randall Daubins . . . his book is called *Satan's Lament*? As in, the movie *Satan's Lament*?"

"You've seen it?"

He shook his head. "My son asked me to take him to it. I did a little research on it, first—the *New Yorker* review was enough for me to know it wasn't appropriate viewing material for him."

"How old is your son?"

"Thirty-five," he said. "I'm glad you like your work at this Broken Angel. You can continue to do it. There. Not here."

"I can't," she said, hating how desperate she sounded. "Harper acquired us this summer. I was let go in September, along with half the editorial staff."

There. Now that she'd said it, she felt better. It wasn't like she'd been fired. She'd been *let go*. It wasn't her fault, but she still felt like she'd been dumped. Her laid-off coworkers had mostly landed on their feet. They were now scattered among the other large corporate publishers, where the right connections and Ivy League credentials guaranteed you a job. For a Midwest girl who had never been that great at playing the game, there were no guarantees. No guarantees, and no interviews.

"That's unfortunate, Miss Meyer," Mr. Blackwood said. "But you're a smart gal. You've done your research. What made you think you were even remotely qualified for this position?"

She dug her nails into her palms. True, Blackwood-Patterson hadn't been her first or even tenth choice. They were old-fashioned, snooty. They pumped out depressing literary fiction about middle-aged men who masturbated and cried. Sometimes, the men also cheated on their wives and cried. So, yeah, she'd applied as a last resort, only after striking out everywhere else. But just because her past was in genre publishing didn't mean she wasn't capable of editing different types of books.

"Cat got your tongue, Miss Meyer?" Mr. Blackwood said. He held her resume up between his thumb and index finger, as if it were a used tissue. "Tell me," he said slowly, enunciating each syllable as if he was talking to a very stupid child, "did you really think you had a shot, when all you've worked on is this . . . tripe?"

"Tripe?" she repeated. Horror was the hottest genre in the industry. The unholy trinity of horror—King, Straub, and Rice—were in a three-way competition to see who could kill the most trees. You'd have to be a fool to not see how commercial "tripe" had become. "Forget my own books. What about *Rosemary's Baby*? Is that 'tripe'? I don't suppose you've even read Shirley Jackson. If you'd only open your eyes—"

He raised a cadaverous hand to silence her. "One need not read a book to make an informed opinion about its content. Just as one does not need to eat McDonald's to know such 'food' is unfit for human consumption."

She straightened her spine. If he was going to be that way, then . . .

"Mr. Blackwood," she began, "you wouldn't know a good book if it walked into your office and . . . and took a bite out of your cold black heart."

They stared at each other for a long beat.

"Young lady," he said finally, "you've been reading too many horror novels. Good day."

Lussi scooted off the chair. She was seething . . . seething and embarrassed. Had she really thought she could convince an old codger like Mr. Blackwood that her track record in the industry was anything more than a joke?

As she spun on her heel to leave, the toe of her Mary Jane caught in a fold of the vast area rug, sending her tumbling, arms splayed, into a bookcase. She caught herself on the lip of an eye-level shelf with her fingertips, but almost immediately fell backward, taking the shelf and its contents with her. She landed on her backside, surrounded by Mr. Blackwood's books and trinkets.

He didn't even lean over the desk to see if she was okay. "Agnes will clean that up," she heard him say in an unperturbed tone.

She sat up. She was uninjured, but thoroughly humiliated. Was this building trying to kill her? She was getting to her feet when a tipped-over black box caught her eye. She turned it right side up, and nearly squealed with delight at what she found underneath the lid.

"Wow," she said, picking up a weathered, handmade doll with strikingly odd features. An electric charge of recognition ran up her spine. "I had one of these when I was a kid. My grandmother brought it over from Germany. It's supposed to drive away evil spirits, right?"

Everything was made of plastic these days. Not Mr. Blackwood's doll. Like Oma's, this one had a torso and appendages fashioned from a long-haired animal pelt. The gray-black fur was matted and gunky with age. Its devil-like face, carved of wood, was just as hideous as the one she remembered, right down to the double set of horns made of polished bone.

Germans were into some strange shit.

No wonder Lussi had grown up to be a horror fan.

"Warding off evil is one of the many . . . unusual properties of the *Perchten*," Mr. Blackwood said, pronouncing the German word like a native speaker. "PAIRK-ten." The plural of *Percht*. Lussi and her sister had never mastered the pronunciation. They'd simply called Oma's doll "Perky."

"I used to make him marry Skipper," Lussi said, lost in her reminiscence. "Barbie had Ken, but poor Skipper was always so lonely. I guess she was only in junior high. Not that Perky—"

"The Perchten are not toys," Mr. Blackwood said, reaching over her shoulder and ripping it away. He stuffed the doll back into its box and set it high on the bookshelf. One of its hairy arms was sticking out from under the lid, as if it didn't want to let her go.

"I'm so sorry, Mr. Blackwood," she stammered. "If I broke any-thing, I'll buy you—"

"Leave," he said, falling back into his chair. He held one hand with the other, failing to mask a slight tremor. Was he shaking from anger, or something else?

There was no point in her saying more. If she wasn't going to get the job before, she certainly wasn't going to now. The man in charge was mercurial. Ill-tempered. Was this what working in the world of dreary, too-serious literary fiction did to you? If so, she'd dodged a silver bullet.

"Thank you for your time," she said, trying to end their meet-ing on a polite note. But something was wrong. Mr. Blackwood's eyes were unfocused, scanning the room wildly. She could see that he was taking sharp breaths in, with no air going back out.

"My . . . pills," he rasped. He slapped a heavy hand on his desk.

She elbowed past his trembling body and rifled through his desk drawer until she found a clear orange prescription bottle. Nitroglycerin. Her heart was beating as hard as it had when she was twelve and stayed up to watch *Night of the Living Dead* for the first time. Her hands were shaking, but she forced them to pry the bottle open.

She pushed a pill into his mouth. "Mr. Blackwood, do you need some water or—"

He grabbed Lussi's forearm, clung to it so hard she knew he was leaving a bruise. "Don't," he said. "Leave me—"

"I won't. Not until an ambulance—"

"No . . . Don't . . . leave me . . . alone with it."

Lussi looked into Mr. Blackwood's eyes. They were filled with terror.

CHAPTER THREE

The next day, Lussi went to see Mr. Blackwood at the NYU Medical Center. The moment she stepped off the elevator and into the intensive-care unit, she knew she'd made a mistake.

She didn't know Xavier Blackwood. Not really. What would his family think of her? Easy—she'd already decided she wouldn't introduce herself. The plan was to drop off the bouquet she'd picked up at the corner bodega and be on her way. But if his secretary was here, she would recognize Lussi from yesterday. Would she think Lussi was trying to suck up to the old man in an attempt to squeeze past the other job candidates?

The thought made her nauseous. That wasn't who she was.

Coming here was a bad idea. She shoved the flowers into the small bronze trash can, hit the down button, and waited. The floor numbers lit up one by one. This was going to take forever—there were fourteen floors, and the elevator seemed to be stopping at every one on its way back to her. Were there stairs? There had to be. If she could just—

A man in a wrinkled suit stubbed out a cigarette on the ashtray on top of the trash can. "I can't believe it," he muttered.

Lussi turned to him. "Are you speaking to me?"

He pointed at a portable cellular phone the size of a high-top tennis shoe pressed to his ear.

"Yeah, Dad's dead," the man said into the phone, turning away from her. "Heart attack. That asshole. What am I supposed to do now? Run the company? Last book I read was *The Great Gatsby*, back in prep school. Stop crying, Mother. Can we focus here?"

Oh God. Xavier Blackwood was dead.

A man she'd practically wished death upon yesterday.

She plucked the bouquet from the trash and followed Mr. Blackwood's son down the hall. She would keep her distance until he finished his phone call. The plan—the new plan—was to give him her condolences, then leave. She'd make it fast.

"You can handle all that funeral bullshit, right? Come on, I know you two have been divorced for twenty years, but seriously. I have a lot on my plate right now." Then, "Great. Thank you. Thanks a lot, Mother. Goodbye."

He punched a button on his phone and mimed throwing it on the ground and stomping on it. He was a pretty good mime.

"Um, Mr. Blackwood?" she said. He looked her up and down. "I just wanted to say I'm so, so sorry for your loss," she said, handing him the flowers. "I couldn't help but overhear your conversation. I just . . . I can't believe he's gone."

He glanced from the bouquet to the elevator at the end of the hall. "Did you get those from the trash?"

She gave him a sheepish grin. "They're carnations. I think."

"Who are you again? You're not with the *Post*, are you? I already threw one of you goons out—"

"Lussi Meyer. Book editor," she said, extending a hand. He looked at it like she'd just had it in the trash can, which, to be fair, was accurate. "I was in your father's office when he . . . uh, when he took ill."

Took ill? When had she turned into Jane Austen?

"Digby Blackwood," he said without shaking her hand. "You must be the girl they told me about. The one who tried to save him. But that's my father for you—stubborn. If he's determined to do something, there's no stopping him."

She could only nod.

"You were interviewing for the open editorial position, right? How'd that go?"

Lussi bit her lip. She hadn't considered that she was the only one who knew how badly her interview had gone. Not even Mr. Blackwood's secretary knew.

"We . . . had a nice chat," she said, skirting the truth.

"Nice? That doesn't sound like Dad."

"We talked about the books I edited. My background is in genre fiction—horror, mainly."

"Anything I'd know?"

"*Satan's Lament?*"

A flicker of recognition. He took a step closer, staring at her intently. "He liked to break people. You hardly seem broken to me."

She tucked a stray hair behind her ear and offered a weak smile. "You don't know me."

"Not yet," he said. There was a mischievous twinkle in his blue eyes that hadn't been there moments ago. He might have been handsome if he didn't have such thick bags under his eyes. And dried blood just under his left nostril. She couldn't imagine the stress of losing a parent. Losing her grandmother had simply wrecked her.

He shook his head. "I wished him dead a billion times, but I didn't mean it. Well, no, I did mean it. But I wanted him dead after he unloaded that book dump off on someone else."

"You don't mean that."

The air between them grew arctic, and for a moment she glimpsed more of the father in his son than she'd noticed before. But then his eyes thawed as quickly as they'd chilled. "I don't have to tell you that the publishing house is in bad shape."

As she'd suspected. "How bad?"

"Put it this way: they're up shit creek and being fucked by the paddle."

"Ouch."

"The company needs a cash infusion before the end of the fiscal year, or it's lights-out at the Blackwood Building. I've been making calls all afternoon. Nobody wants to put up a dime. Every conversation is the same: *Oh, you're a publisher? Anything I might have read?* They don't care about Dad's Pulitzers. If they haven't seen people reading our books on airplanes, then we're worthless." He ran both hands through his hair, pulling on the curly locks until they stood on end. "I'm sorry, I don't know why I'm telling you this. It's my problem, not yours."

He was on the verge of tears. A wreck, drifting on an ocean of despair. She wanted to help him . . . but how? An idea slowly began to form, first a blur, but growing more concrete by the moment. Perhaps . . . perhaps there was a way they could help each other.

She cleared her throat. "Forgive me if this comes off as crass . . . but did Mr. Blackwood tell anyone that he'd come to a decision about the open job? Before he passed. Which I'm so, so sorry about, by the way."

Digby shook his head. "He was in and out of it. Why do you ask?"

"I wasn't being honest with you earlier."

"Oh. Do tell . . ."

"You were right about my interview—it wasn't a nice chat. It was brutal. Your father trashed my record in the industry, all because he didn't think there was any value in books about vampires and werewolves and interdimensional, soul-sucking leeches. Ask any bookseller what their hottest-selling genre is right now. Then try telling me there's no 'value' in horror. The cold, hard fact is that Blackwood-Patterson hasn't had a real blockbuster since Carter was in office. Meanwhile, all I do is shit best sellers."

Digby raised an eyebrow. This, from the paddle-fucking guy.

"The company is yours now. Not his," Lussi said, on a roll. "I understand if you want to redo all the interviews, or just leave the open position unfilled . . . but if things are really as bad as you say, then you can't afford to waste time. What you need is somebody who can find you the next Stephen King."

She paused to catch her breath. When he didn't say anything right away, she worried she'd gone too far. His father was dead, and now some strange, excitable girl had him cornered in the hospital hallway, trying to talk her way into a job. She either had to apologize now, or pull the fire alarm and run.

Digby's face relaxed. "Fine. Pay is . . . I don't know. Whatever you make at your current job plus ten percent?" She could only nod. She felt like she was going to throw up the egg salad she'd eaten for lunch. "Good. Just let my dad's payroll director know. Whoever that is. I'm sure there's one at the office. The receptionist will tell you where to go."

"So . . . I'm hired?" Her voice climbed to the top of her vocal range.

"We'll make it official Monday—I'll introduce you at the editorial meeting that morning," he said. "Or is Monday too soon?"

She shook her head. It was less than a week from now. That would give him time to settle in. While he was in a giving mood, she decided to push a little further. "Any chance I could talk you into making this a senior position? The ad in *Publishers Weekly* didn't really specify, but I've been at the same level for four years . . ."

"It's a temp position is what it is, if you don't find me the next Stephen McQueen."

"King. Stephen King."

"Find me another *him* by New Year's, and you're my new best friend. But fine. Senior editor. Whatever."

"Wait. Did you say the end of this month? It takes eighteen months, minimum, from contract to publication date. If I had a manuscript ready to go right now, we could rush it through for next fall. Maybe. But what you're suggesting—"

"I'm not an idiot," he said. "The end of the calendar year is also the end of Blackwood's fiscal year. I'm not asking you to publish the book in the next three weeks, or even in the next three years. I don't care if it's ever published, frankly. What I need is to finish this year with a surefire best seller under contract. If this company is going to survive long enough for me to turn it around, I need to project value, not just dusty prestige."

This was crazy. She was going to walk into the Blackwood Building with a target on her back. Not only would she likely be the youngest senior editor on staff, but she had a mandate at odds with everything the swan logo on the spine of every Black-wood-Patterson book stood for. Why had she opened her big mouth?

The task itself was also crazy, but not impossible. Almost nobody in publishing worked in December. That gave her an advantage. Manuscripts were piling up on editors' and agents' desks all around town. Editors at other houses wouldn't be making offers on new books until after the holidays. If she found a diamond in the slush pile, there was less chance that it had already been scooped up by another publisher. With her first couple of paychecks, she could begin paying her half of the rent again. There was even an outside chance of flying home to Iowa for Christmas, which she'd all but written off.

"I'll do it," she said, brimming with confidence. "I won't let you down."

She held out her free hand. He still hadn't accepted the bouquet, but he took her palm in his with an unexpected tenderness. "See you next Monday morning. Nine a.m. sharp. Or whatever time publishing starts. Now if you'll excuse me . . ."

He turned his attention to his mobile phone and began to wander down the hall. Before he could dial, she called out to him. "Wait," she said. "How will you know I've found the next Stephen King?"

"Easy. All you have to do is find me something so good even I would want to read it."

If he'd left it there, her job would have been relatively easy, all things considered. She could guess what would appeal to a man like Digby: Blood and guts, no big words. Frequent chapter breaks. A little sex (nothing weird). Unfortunately, he had one last directive: "Not that I'm actually going to read it. I don't have that sort of time. We'll run it past the editor in chief. Get her to sign off on it, and we're in business."

CHAPTER FOUR

Knowing some staff might still be in mourning on her first day, Lussi paired her black blouse with a sober gray blazer and black slacks. She combed her bangs down instead of fluffing them. A man was dead—this was not the time nor place for Aqua Net. She took one last look in the mirror behind her door before leaving. To her dismay, she still looked like she hadn't slept a wink last night. Which was exactly what had happened. But still.

She'd spent all yesterday pounding yeast in the tiny kitchen of her Staten Island apartment. It had been years since she'd made stollen from her grandmother's recipe. She'd forgotten how violent the process was. How had Oma managed it every year with her arthritis? The woman had baked a dozen or more of the German fruitcakes every holiday season, and Lussi had never heard her complain once.

Lussi wanted to make an impression on her first day at Blackwood-Patterson. It was especially important that she start off on the right foot with the editor in chief, Mary Beth Wilkerson. Otherwise known as "The Raven." The woman had a reputation as one of the hardest-nosed editors in the business . . . and she held Lussi's future in the palm of her hand, whether she knew it or not.

Oma used to say the way to a man's heart was through his stomach. Hopefully, home-baked goods could work on women, too. The idea for a traditional stollen had popped into her head after seeing the Percht in Mr. Blackwood's office. The doll had brought back warm feelings of Christmases past at Oma's house. It felt like kismet.

Or a recipe for disaster. Lussi had forgotten that stollen was a multiday process, and attempted to cram it into a single day. By the time she finally pulled the loaf out of the oven, it was around four in the morning. No sooner had she fallen asleep, it seemed, than her alarm-clock had begun ringing.

Well, she thought, staring at her tired reflection in the mirror, *that's why Baby Jesus invented coffee.*

Lussi arrived at the Blackwood Building at a quarter to nine. Every cell in her body was buzzing. Maybe it was the extra cup of coffee. (It was the extra cup of coffee.) The receptionist—Gail, who actually did have a lovely paisley-print Vera Bradley stashed under her desk—led her up the winding staircase. They stopped on the second floor so Lussi could drop her fruitcake in the fridge. It hadn't quite cooled yet. She only had a brief moment to take in the break room, but it was pretty standard. Sink filled with unwashed coffee mugs? Check. Round Formica tables surrounded by spindly chairs? Check. Fridge that was too small for a staff of twenty-five? Check.

"Lunch?" Gail asked, pouring herself a coffee.

"It's for the editorial meeting," Lussi said. She squeezed her fruitcake into the fridge between the Ziploc bags of sandwiches and Tupperware containers. "Would you like me to bring you some after the meeting? It's homemade."

Gail blew on her coffee. "I'm on Nutri/System."

On the third floor, Gail led her down a long hall. She paused at a door plastered in comics clipped from newspapers. "This is the art department. If the door is closed, that means Stanley doesn't want to be disturbed. I'm sure you've worked with artists before—you know how easily they startle."

Gail stopped at the end of the hall at a bare door with unfinished wood. The key used to unlock it was black and rusted. The door creaked open, letting out a foul, stale odor. The walls were white . . . at some point. The office was empty except for the basics. It was the "new employee" starter kit: desk, chair, phone, a pair of bookshelves, and a short, gun-metal-gray filing cabinet. The carpet had more stains than the floor of a Times Square peep show.

Lussi opened the blinds. Sunlight poured in, causing her to shield her eyes. When she adjusted the angle of the blinds, though—oh, the view! Her office faced the street, which meant she could see the entirety of the park. It would be gorgeous come spring . . . if she was still here. And if the city cleared the tents.

She turned to ask Gail where the bathroom was, but the woman had already gone. Well, fine. Lussi didn't need to pee. Yet.

She set her tote bag on her desk. It had everything she needed for Day One at her new job: her *Phantom of the Opera* coffee mug, which she'd won in a radio contest along with a pair of preview tickets. Plastic vampire fangs (a cheesy gift from an ex-coworker). A box of #2 Ticonderoga pencils—black, because you don't edit horror novels with "a god-damned buttercup-yellow pencil, Lussi," as the legendary Sandy Chainsaw once told her. And, of course, a half dozen books she'd worked on. Even though they were from her former publisher, they were still her babies. You didn't just drown your kids in the river when you left your husband. Although, admittedly, some mothers did.

Oh, how she wished she had access to the talented roster she'd put together at Broken Angel. That would have made the task Digby assigned her much easier. Unfortunately, Harper & Row had most of her old authors locked up with multibook deals and option clauses. This was a new start. A clean break from the past. A thought both terrifying and thrilling. Luckily, those were her two favorite emotions.

The phone line to Xavier's secretary kept going to her an-swering machine. Lussi didn't want to go upstairs unannounced—protocol seemed super important at Blackwood-Patterson—so she decided to take a few minutes to find out where the company kept their submissions. It wasn't always the best avenue for finding new authors, but it was a start.

Things were quieter this morning than last week. Most of the office doors were closed, muffling any typewriter clicking and clacking that might have been going on. Every once in a while, she'd hear a deep cough from somewhere in the building.

She peeked into the first open door she came across. The room was double the size of her office, but windowless. There were three desks pushed up against the walls, each one occupied by a middle-aged man, all with varying degrees of hair loss. The fluorescent desk lamps did them no favors. They looked like a bunch of zombies with liver disease. She wondered when the last time any of them had gone on a date, or even seen sunlight.

These were her people. It felt good to be back in publishing.

She walked over to the closest zombie, a round fellow with a ponytail and what looked like a fleck of salami in his beard. Definitely a meat product. "Excuse me? Hello?" Lussi said, leaning slightly forward to catch his attention.

He was in deep concentration, marking up a manuscript page. Copy edits, from the look of it. It took him a second to realize she was there . . . but when he did look up, he kicked his feet in surprise, pushing his chair back three feet and taking him with it.

"Whoa, it's okay," she said, raising her hands in surrender. Neither of the other two guys even turned at the commotion. "I come in peace."

He slapped his hand over his chest, panting. "Sorry, sorry," he said, wheeling himself back to his desk. "I just . . . whew, don't scare a guy like that."

"Sorry." She smiled sheepishly. "I edit horror novels. Scaring people is sort of what I do."

"Funny," he said without smiling. "We don't publish that stuff."

"Well, you do now," she said. Clearly, the company grapevine didn't reach this office. Copy editors tended to be lone wolves. Probably because whenever you cornered one, you could tell they were silently judging your grammar. "I'm the new senior editor. Lussi Meyer. I interviewed with Mr. Blackwood. Xavier, I mean. Before he passed."

"If you say so." He held out his hand, thick fingers covered in red ink. "I'm Joe, but everyone calls me Sloppy Joe. Copy editor to the stars."

"I'm sorry, did you say 'Sloppy' . . ."

"I left a comma out of a Muriel Spark novel in 1963," he said with the hundred-yard stare of a man who had seen and done terrible things. "Changed the whole meaning of the sentence . . ."

"You're kidding."

He shook his head. "But it's a good place to work. I like it, at least. Always plenty of parking around here, if you have a car." He frowned. "I don't have a car."

She let go of his hand. "You wouldn't, by any chance, know where I can find the slush pile? And the ladies' room."

"Why would you want to go there?"

Because I have to pee so bad I can taste it, she almost said, before realizing he was asking why she wanted to see the slush pile.

"Digby wants me to find him a best seller, and that's where I thought I'd start. I would guess nobody reads the horror submissions. You all have a slush pile, right?"

"We do . . . but we don't talk about it."

"Because . . ."

"We used to have an intern who read for us," he said, his voice low. "They left a while ago. The manuscripts have been piling up since then. Half a dozen come in over the transom every day. Never mind the fact that we're not even open to unsolicited submissions—it says right there in *Writer's Market.* I can show you the page."

"That's okay," Lussi said. "So what happens to all these manuscripts?"

"They're all in storage. In the basement." He pulled the salami from his beard, looked at it as if trying to remember the last time he'd had salami, then ate it. "Take a flashlight," he whispered to her. "It's spooky down there."

CHAPTER FIVE

Lussi's finely honed publishing instincts told her the base-
ment was probably going to be downstairs. The winding staircase
stopped in the lobby, but she found a service elevator not far from
it. Unfortunately, there was a hand-drawn OUT OF ORDER sign
taped to the metal door. Somebody had added a crude drawing
of a tombstone. Lussi read the grave marker's inscription out loud:
"R.I.P. Frederick."

Maybe the elevator's name was Frederick, she thought.

She was about to ask Gail for directions when she spied a metal
FALLOUT SHELTER sign next to an unmarked door off to the side.
The door opened onto a staircase descending into darkness. She
pulled an overhead chain, and a single, low-watt bulb blinkered
on. She almost wished she hadn't turned it on. The planks on the
stairs were so old that footsteps had worn down the middles to
bare wood. The handrail looked like it had been chewed on by . . .
something. The railing was shot through with splinters, making it
impossible to use as support.

Lussi took the stairs one at a time, steadying herself against
the brick walls, which seemed to grow closer together the farther
down she went. The boards sagged under her weight. What would

happen if Sloppy Joe, a man three times her size, attempted to make the trek into the basement? She knew the answer to that: an OUT OF ORDER sign, graffitied with another gravestone.

She found another light switch at the bottom of the stairs. The overhead fluorescents flickered to life, waking a gang of roaches huddled around a floor drain. They scattered for cover. Lussi was sorry to upset their little powwow, but not upset to see them go. They were twice the size of the ones at her apartment.

She hadn't brought a flashlight, but there was more than enough light. Metal shelving extended a hundred feet or so in every direction. Boxes were stacked haphazardly, both on the shelves and on the damp cement floor. Spooky? The spookiest thing about the basement was how much it reminded her of the Staten Island Mini-Storage where she kept the worldly possessions she couldn't cram into a New York City apartment. (Basically everything she owned.) She wiped dust off the closest cardboard box to read the label. TAXES 1955.

Along the far wall were a series of ten-by-ten cages with chain-link fencing on all sides, reinforced with wooden beams. Perhaps they'd once kept sticky-fingered staff out of office supplies, but they were no longer padlocked. Now they housed unused holiday decorations, shrink-wrapped pallets of overstock books, and—just what she was looking for—stuffed envelopes and loose manuscripts towering all the way to the unfinished ceiling. The slush pile.

Lussi stepped inside the cage with the stacked manuscripts. As soon as she let go of the door, it swung closed behind her with a snap, like a triggered mouse trap. She jumped half an inch. Good to know her reflexes were still working.

The shortest stacks topped out around her shoulders, so that's where she would start her search. It was a gold mine just waiting to be panned. She began flipping through the manuscripts one by one. The unpublished authors addressed their letters to Mr. Black-wood and other editors at the house, begging, pleading for a book contract. Sloppy Joe hadn't been clear whether anyone sent out rejection letters, or if these poor authors were still waiting on pins and needles to hear back from the prestigious publishing house. Either way, there wasn't a cent of return postage. Some destitute editorial assistant had been absconding with the stamps authors included for their manuscripts' safe return.

The third submission she looked at was a horror novel. *In Dog We Trust*. Promising title. She read the first line: *Last Thursday night was the first time I saw the werewolf pissing on my grandmother's grave.*

Getting it past Blackwood-Patterson's formidable editor in chief would be an uphill battle, but it sure beat the hell out of "Call me Ishmael."

It wasn't the only horror novel. In fact, for a literary publisher, there were a surprising number of horror submissions. It made some sense, what with the explosion of the horror market over the past decade. She began setting them aside, but soon realized she was building her own tower of manuscripts—thirteen or fourteen. And that was just from the one stack, so far. She'd about reached the limit of what she could safely carry up those rickety steps in one go. She hoisted what she had up into her arms and was about to head for the stairs when the lights went out.

"Hey, there's somebody down here," she shouted. The darkness was absolute. "Hello? Could you turn the lights back on?"

No answer. She listened for footsteps on the stairs, but all she could hear was a flood of water rushing through the pipes over-head. When that finished, the quiet returned. She called out for help again and again, her voice a little louder each time. If only she'd brought a flashlight like the copy editor had insisted . . .

Of course. They were hazing the new girl. How could she have been so blind? Sloppy Joe's hushed "warning" had been a bit too melodramatic. Nice try, guys, but she was no stranger to hazing. Her first day at Broken Angel, her coworkers had locked her inside a storage closet with a clown. "Seven Minutes in Hell," they'd called it. There had been whiskey on the clown's breath—cheap whiskey. Fortunately, the clown passed out within thirty seconds. There was no way they could have known she'd always had an irrational fear of clowns. But that day, clutching a mop for protection in case the drunk woke up, she learned that she'd never really been afraid of clowns. What scared her were the men underneath the pancake makeup.

God, she missed the Broken Angel crew. They'd had a lot of fun together.

"Hazing the new girl, ha-ha," she said, projecting her voice more forcefully this time. "You can turn the lights back on. Anytime now would be great."

Lussi waited, but heard nothing. No giggles. No footsteps.

Were they really going to leave her in the dark? Okay, then. Her eyes had adjusted as much as they were going to. It would have to be enough. Only a sliver of natural light filtered through the windows, which were boarded up with plywood. She'd heard once that pigeons could find their way home blindfolded. She was smarter than a pigeon. Probably.

Manuscripts in hand, she nudged the cage door with her foot. It didn't open. She jammed her shoulder into the crisscrossed wire. It refused to give under her weight. Groaning, she set her load down and tried the door again, this time grounding her legs and pressing into it with her arms. It was stuck. She slipped her fingers through the wire, felt for the door handle. There was no latch, inside or out. No lock.

It didn't make sense.

"Open up, open up, open up," she hissed, rattling the door harder. The air seemed to have cooled off, as if somebody had shut off the building's heat. She stopped shaking the door and started counting backward from one hundred in her head. It was a technique her analyst said would help her quell anxiety. Slowly, as she hit ninety, then eighty, then seventy, her breathing began to return to normal.

She was not alone. She sensed someone watching her from the darkness. She couldn't see them—couldn't hear them—but they were there beyond her field of vision, swallowing up the silence itself.

She rattled the door again, but felt even more resistance this time. It was like someone was holding it closed from the other side, which made no sense—she could see through the chain-link, and there was no one there. And yet . . .

Her thoughts were drowned out by a whispering voice that seemed to come from everywhere and nowhere all at once. *Hunger.*

"You're hungry?" Lussi said, backing away from the door. "I don't understand. Who's hungry? Let me out, please, please just let me—"

That's when she heard the unmistakable sound of the door being ripped off the front of one of the cages. She heard boxes tumble over, and then, to her absolute horror, she saw a glowing white figure hovering in midair in the next cage over.

Whatever came out of her mouth next was involuntary and almost certainly unintelligible. In fact, she hadn't even been aware she was capable of issuing such high-pitched sounds. The rational part of her brain was trying to calm her panic—there had to be an absolutely, perfectly reasonable explanation for all of this.

The emotional part was running in circles, naked and howling.

The overhead lights came back on. This snapped her back to

reality long enough for her to shake the door again. "I'm back here! I'm stuck in a cage!" She gave the door one last good kick and the wooden frame splintered, releasing the door and sending her hurtling out of the cage. She landed hard on her hip.

Heart still pounding, she whipped around to face the ghost. And indeed, it was a ghost—the kind you put in your front yard in October, as the days grow short and the leaves change colors. A glow-in-the-dark blow-up mold, propped up on a card table.

She took a moment to catch her breath.

What the hell just happened?

Digby rounded the corner and stopped when he saw her on the floor. "Listen, I'll have to call you back . . . Hello? Hello?" He looked at his cellular phone. "Lost him." He glanced from Lussi to the broken cage doors, then back at Lussi. She imagined her face was frozen in the twisted shape of that Edvard Munch painting, *The Scream*.

"So, ah, how's your first day going?" Digby asked.

CHAPTER SIX

Lussi was worried that Digby would think she was crazy, but he was too preoccupied to ask why she'd been screaming. He just seemed glad she 'wasn't hurt. He promised to find someone to cart the manuscripts up to her office. He was about to tackle several file boxes of financial records, he explained. "I'll also have Alan look at the service elevator. The last thing we need is for someone to break their neck on those stairs," he said, pulling a box from atop a shelf. "One lawsuit, and this whole operation comes crashing down."

"Have him look at the lights as well, if you could," she said, still a bit shaken.

"I already know what he'll say: *It's an old building.* That's all he ever says. Laziest maintenance man I've ever dealt with. I'd let him go if I could, but supposedly he has, like, ten kids to support." Digby continued to move boxes around. "I'll wait until after the holidays."

Lussi nodded. "Do you want me to leave word with Agnes to remind you to speak to Alan?"

He shook his head. "No use. I fired her last week."

Lussi stared at him, perplexed. In their brief interactions before and after the disastrous interview, Mr. Blackwood's personal secretary had seemed both kind and competent. She also seemed like the type of woman who knew where the bodies were buried. In short: invaluable.

Digby caught her look. "Don't worry. My father set her up for life. She'll live out the rest of her days in her palatial Massapequa estate, living far better than the rest of us."

Lussi didn't know what to say, so she just gave him a little wave goodbye and went upstairs empty-handed. As she mounted the spiral staircase, she saw a trio of young women entering the second-floor conference room. Lussi checked her watch. Eleven on the nose. The editorial meeting was about to start. How had she spent over an hour in the basement? It didn't seem possible. No time to head to the fridge for her fruitcake, or even to process everything that just happened in the basement.

She dashed down the hallway as fast as her short legs would allow. A tall man holding the door let out a shriek as she barreled toward him. She slowed to a fast walk as she reached the door. "Sorry," she said, her quads on fire.

She took a seat at the far end of the conference table. The woman with the buzz cut from the morning of her interview was seated at the head of the table. The Raven. No wonder Lussi hadn't recognized her from afar—the editor in chief's trademark black hair had been almost completely shorn off. The other three women at the table—editors, all in their mid to late thirties, Lussi guessed—were dressed alike in striped polyester power suits with pointed shoulders. Their dark hair was swept up into matching high side-ponies. Before Lussi had applied for the job, she'd been warned by an ex-coworker that the Blackwood-Patterson employees were a different sort of strange. What else did you expect from the East Village, though? He said it went deeper than that. "They're like V. C. Andrews characters," he'd said.

She was beginning to see what he meant. This trio looked like they'd spent their whole childhoods together in an attic.

The man holding the door open poked his head back out to see if anyone else was about to make a surprise appearance. Satisfied that the coast was clear, he shut the door and took the seat next to Lussi. His face was as long as the rest of him, as if someone had stamped out his features on Silly Putty and stretched it.

The room was silent. All eyes were on Lussi, waiting for her to either explain her presence or leave. *Shit or get off the pot, girl.*

Oh, how she wished she had her fruitcake.

"I'm Lussi," she said, forcing a smile. "The new—"

"You have a spider in your hair," the woman seated directly across from her said.

Lussi rolled her eyes up but couldn't see through her bangs. She had no fear of creepy-crawlies—she'd collected insects one summer, until her parents found the plastic milk jug with breathing holes under her bed. That didn't mean she wanted a creepy-crawly in her hair. She bent over the side of her chair and brushed her hair out with her fingers. A daddy longlegs tumbled to the carpet. Each of its legs was a long, impossibly thin fishhook. It scrambled up and over a chrome mechanical pencil and then went straight for The Raven's feet.

Lussi picked up the pencil and sat back up. "Did someone drop this?"

The man sitting next to her snatched it away without a word. He shot Lussi an evil side-eye and flared his nostrils.

"Okay, then," she said. "As I was saying, I'm Lussi. The new senior editor."

Nervous glances were tossed in The Raven's direction.

The editor in chief made direct eye contact with Lussi. Her gaze was so piercing, Lussi had to look away, lest she be turned to stone. "Thank you for joining us, Ms. Meyer. We'll go quickly around the room and introduce ourselves. We've got a lot to cover today. Let's start on my left, with . . ."

Each of the women spoke in turn so quickly that their names went in one of Lussi's ears and out the other. She picked up on the fact that they were all a level or two below her. She still couldn't believe she'd talked Digby into handing her a senior editorship. Not that she felt bad about it. Home-grown editors were rarely rewarded for their loyalty. The best way to get ahead was to get out.

The tall man seated next to Lussi introduced himself last. "Stanley Kenward O'Connell," he said with a laconic drawl. "Art director." She waited for more, but that was his entire spiel.

Lussi was up next. She took a big inhale—when she was any sort of nervous, she tended to speak rapidly and run out of air—but The Raven stepped in. "Thank you everyone for sharing," she said. "Let's get down to business. We're running behind already."

The editorial trio shared updates on their current projects. They showered each other with praise, and occasionally completed each other's sentences. Lussi didn't think the trio's cohesion was solely for her benefit. Their hive mind was too well lubricated. Thirteen minutes into the meeting, Lussi settled on a pet name for them: Dracula's Brides.

No question who Dracula was. How was Lussi going to get a book—any book—past The Raven? Every time Lussi attempted to speak, the editor in chief quieted her with a look of utter disdain. The reason wasn't hard to guess: Digby had hired Lussi without consulting her. Every office had its own protocols, but you'd be hard-pressed to find one where the top-ranking editor didn't have at least some input into new hires. The only reason she hadn't sat in on Lussi's interview with Mr. Blackwood was because the old man hadn't wanted to waste his highest-paid staffer's precious time.

If only Lussi had her stollen to soften the woman up.

Stanley passed around some cover mock-ups for a new Richard Yates short story collection. There wasn't much enthusiasm in the room for any of them. "Just pick one," The Raven said. "Somebody, please. This needs to be at the printer last week."

When nobody wanted to go out on a limb, Lussi raised her hand.

Five pairs of eyes turned to her. "I like the third one. With the wheelbarrow. Maybe it could have, I don't know, a little more personality, though?"

Dracula's Brides exchanged looks of disbelief. The Raven smiled at Lussi. "And how, pray tell, would you go about giving a wheelbarrow 'more personality'?"

Stanley rubbed his chin. "I could see—"

The Raven cut him off with a raised palm.

"Well," Lussi said, "maybe it could have some dirt in it? Go more rustic. It looks like it's never been used. Or, you could go in a different direction with, I don't know . . . a skull?"

She didn't know why she'd said it. She'd wanted to contribute something, anything to the meeting, to prove her worth, to show them she deserved to be here. Unfortunately, her mouth had been running faster than her brain. She'd forgotten where she was. A skull? Jesus Christ, what was she now, thirteen?

As the seconds audibly ticked away on her watch, nobody breathed. Nobody sniffled, nobody bounced a foot under the table, nobody scratched an itch, nobody so much as blinked.

Finally, one of Dracula's Brides cleared her throat. "I like it."

"A skull would certainly be different," Bride #3 said, nodding.

"What if it scares people?" Bride #2 said.

"It's a dark book," Bride #1 said. "Remember *Revolutionary Road*? That ended with the wife killing herself and her unborn baby. This one ends with a *quintuple* murder-suicide."

Bride #3 shook her head. "That's sad."

"So sad," Bride #2 said. "So, so sad."

The Raven never took her eyes off Lussi. When the editors had finished their little debate, The Raven told Stanley to do a mock-up of the new concept. "But we need it by the end of day. Go. Now." He scooped up his drawings—and his beloved pencil—and left in a flurry.

The Raven snapped her day planner shut. "Our time is up. I'll schedule a follow-up on the Yates book tomorrow. And don't forget—if you haven't left your Secret Santa gift under the tree downstairs, do it soon. The party's this Friday."

"Did you already draw names?" Lussi asked, pushing her chair out.

"Two weeks ago, I'm afraid," The Raven said. "Everybody's name was in there . . . except for yours." She smiled faintly.

"Are you sure?" Bride #2 cut in. "She has a gift under the tree."

The Raven, holding the door open for everyone, dropped her smile. "I made the list—I know whose names were on it," she said. "It sounds like somebody decided to appoint themselves as your Secret Santa, Lussi."

The thought of somebody taking it upon themselves to "welcome" her with an anonymous gift made her uneasy. She was starting to get the feeling that someone had it in for her at the company. Whatever had happened to her in the basement had been a prank. Even if she couldn't explain how they'd pulled it off. Digby had too much going on to waste time pranking her, but there were nearly two dozen other people in the building . . . every one of them a suspect. What in the name of all that was holy was waiting for her under the tree?

CHAPTER SEVEN

The shopping mall below the World Trade Center was bright and airy, with piped-in Christmas tunes and a decorated spruce in the atrium. Despite being a rather frigid Thursday evening, the mall was alive with foot traffic. Most shoppers were well-dressed men with slicked-back hair—brokers who worked in the Financial District, getting a little Christmas shopping done before taking the train back to the 'burbs. The Sears bags were for their wives; the Victoria's Secret bags, for their secretaries.

Lussi hadn't come to the mall to shop, however. One of her Broken Angel authors, Fabien Nightingale, was signing at Waldenbooks. After a long, at times frustrating, first week at the office—which wasn't even over yet—it would be nice to see a familiar face.

After the editorial meeting, the rest of the week had passed without incident. Hardly anyone spoke to her, though she was on the receiving end of several dirty looks from Dracula's Brides and seemed to run into Sloppy Joe every time she went on break. She wanted more one-on-one time with Digby, but he was always either on the phone, walking around with men in dark suits, or holed up in the basement rifling through file boxes. She didn't even pretend to hope for a meeting with The Raven; she'd need to give that relationship some time to grow.

Thankfully, Digby had arranged for someone to bring up the manuscripts from the basement on Monday afternoon. Lussi had returned to her office after lunch—the world's saddest hot dog from the world's saddest park vendor, hastily eaten on the world's saddest street corner—and found stacks and stacks of manuscripts on the floor of her office. But after only three days of reading sub-missions, she was about ready to throw in the towel on the slush pile. One yellowing cover letter was dated 1972. It occurred to Lussi that she might not find the next Stephen King . . . she might find *the* Stephen King. A pre-*Carrie* submission. A Bachman book!

As they say, though, there's more than one way to skin a corpse. She'd begun ringing up every agent in her Rolodex, putting out word that she was on the hunt for fresh talent. The quality of agen-ted submissions compared to slush was night and day. She could hear the skepticism in the agents' voices, though, when she men-tioned her new employer. That was one barrier she should have foreseen. A few promised to overnight her a hot manuscript or two, but so far she hadn't received any mail. How long did it take the post office to deliver a package from Midtown?

Lussi passed a Kay-Bee Toy & Hobby, where a mechanical bear whirred to life. "Hi there, I'm Teddy Ruxpin," it chirped, its eyelids clacking open and shut, open and shut. "Can you and I be friends?"

I don't even see the friends I've got, she thought. Her niece might like the bear, however. She'd have to check with her sister to see if she had one already, or was getting one from Santa. It was looking less and less likely Lussi would be going home for the holidays, however.

She finally found the bookstore. A bored-looking high schooler was reading a Batman comic behind the checkout desk. There were no signs posted for the signing. "Am I in the right place for the Fabien Nightingale event?" Lussi asked. "British gent, bushy mustache . . ."

The kid didn't look up. He pointed to the back of the store.

"Thanks for your help," she said.

"Whatever, lady."

Usually, bookstores set up signing tables near the front of the store to take advantage of foot traffic. Fabien's table was sandwiched between a bookshelf and the fire exit—as far from the store entrance as you could get. A pallet stacked with several dozen copies of Fabien's new book sat next to the table. Lussi had originally had big hopes for *The Night Cathedral*. Fabien had come a long way from his days writing novelizations for B-movies such as *Don't Tread on Jessica's Grave*. However, the market had recently taken a sharp turn away from Fabien's particular brand of quiet horror. Things had gotten bloody. Editors could keep pace with changing trends. Authors, on the other hand . . .

Lussi looked at her watch. She was ten minutes early. Fabien wasn't even here yet, so she hung back, scanning the horror section. She pulled the new Stephen King off the shelves. *It* was the big book of the moment—literally. She'd read the first couple hundred pages in galleys, thanks to a friend at Viking. She still had three-quarters of the book to go.

She had just found the page she'd left off on when her senses were overwhelmed with a thick, cloying fragrance she knew all too well.

"Boo."

She jumped—just a little—and turned. It was, of course, Fabien Nightingale, who traveled in a cloud of Obsession for Men.

"Limey bastard," she said, swatting him in the upper arm with the doorstop of a book, which landed harder than she'd intended. "Next time, say hi like a normal person."

"Didn't think you'd come," he said, rubbing his arm. "And I resent that remark. Never call me a normal person again."

"Why wouldn't I come?" she asked.

"You never returned my RSVP, so I figured you must have other plans," he said. "Besides, we both know publishing's a ghost town around the holidays."

"Things have been crazy," she said. "With the job search and all. Good news, though—"

He pried the book from her hands and examined it, front and back. Fabien was rocking the satanic preacher look tonight: black suit, black button-down shirt, red tie. Black was slimming, but it could only do so much for his beer gut.

He handed the book back with a derisive snort.

"What?" Lussi said.

"I hate clowns."

"Join the club," she said. "There's almost, like, this primal fear of clowns, buried deep in our subconscious. Pennywise is kind of fun, though."

"I meant the other clown . . . Steve."

"Keep your voice down," she whispered.

"You're afraid he's going to come after me?" Fabien said. "Ha. I could take him in a fight. Only one of us knows *karate*."

The last literary titan who could throw a decent punch had been Hemingway. Nobody wanted to see two writers square off in a ring. Though she would pay good money to see Nora Roberts and Janet Dailey go at it.

Lussi steered the conversation into safer waters. She gave Fabien the rundown on her new gig at Blackwood-Patterson. He seemed to make a point of not congratulating her. "Be careful," he warned her. "I've heard things about the old git who runs that place. He can be a little frisky with the young ladies, if you catch my drift.

There are stories about that building. Rumors, mostly, but where there's smoke . . ."

"You haven't heard?"

He shot her a confused look. "About . . . ?"

"Xavier Blackwood," she said. "He's dead."

"Huh." Fabien shrugged. "Bully for you, then. Did he keel over at his desk?"

"How'd you know?"

"It's how all those old literary geezers die. They don't retire— they expire. They work themselves to death. Literally. It's never too early to be thinking about an exit strategy."

"I just started there Monday."

He laughed. "Lussi, dear Lussi . . . I was talking about an exit strategy from this cruel, cruel world."

—

Fifteen minutes passed, then twenty. At the half-hour mark, Lussi could tell that Fabien was ready to throw in the towel. The signing was a bust. Only one person had even approached the table, and they'd asked for directions to the restroom. Fabien, without missing a beat, had pointed to the stacked books beside the table. "The loo's right here," he said.

Right as it looked like Fabien's soul was ready to leave his body and drift away like a shopping bag caught in the breeze, an honest-to-goodness reader finally arrived. The woman was old enough to be Fabien's mother, and she was hauling behind her a rolling suitcase filled with yellowed copies of what looked like his entire oeuvre. Fabien offered the woman his chair, which she gladly accepted. "Can I interest you in a copy of my new book?" he said, handing it to her. "It's my best work yet. But don't take my word for it—ask my editor. She's right here."

The woman examined Lussi's face, as if searching for some hidden sign as to whether or not she should trust this strange young woman. "I don't trust anyone under thirty," the lady said.

Fabien got to work signing her stack of books. Lussi wandered the store for a few minutes. When she returned, Fabien was squatting beside the old woman, who wasn't moving. A tuft of her white hair was gently waving back and forth, caught in a cross breeze from the overhead heating vent. *The Night Cathedral* was splayed open in her lap.

"Bollocks, it's happened again," Fabien said.

"Everything okay?" Lussi asked, drawing in closer. "I know CPR. At least I used to."

Fabien placed a hand to the woman's neck to check for a pulse. After a tense moment in which no one seemed to inhale or exhale, including, troublingly, the woman, Fabien got to his feet. "Sleeping," he said. "Third one this tour."

Lussi put a supportive hand on his shoulder. "I'm sure it's not the book that's putting them to sleep," she said, lying through her teeth. "It's a little slow, but that's by design. It's probably way past her bedtime."

He narrowed his eyes at her but said nothing. He slipped into his oversized gray fur coat. It was quitting time, apparently.

"How about a drink?" he asked, producing a flask. He offered it to her. "Ladies first."

She unscrewed the cap and gagged.

"Absinthe," he said.

"I know what it is," she said, handing it back without imbibing. "The stuff van Gogh was drinking when he cut off his ear. You told me you were done with this stuff."

Fabien took a long swig. When he was finished, he scowled.

"When did I say that?"

"Last year," she said. "That fantasy convention in Cleveland. I found you hungover, on the bathroom floor of your suite with an empty bottle of absinthe lying next to you. And you said—and I quote—'I am done with this shit.' It took six of your little red friends just to get you upright for the panel."

"What I meant was that I was done with Cleveland. Not absinthe—*Cleveland*."

All of the best authors had a touch of madness. When it manifested itself on the page, it was hailed as genius. When it caused them to go on drunken benders for days or weeks at a stretch, it could land them in a halfway house. She wasn't sure which direction Fabien's madness would take him. Lussi couldn't leave him to his own devices tonight, though. Not after an event like this.

"You up for dinner or dessert?" she said. The elderly woman was snoring now; they'd let the bookseller deal with her. "There's a Baskin-Robbins in the food court—"

"There's a pub around the corner," Fabien said, a twinkle in his eyes. His thick black mustache curled up at the edges as he grinned, making him look like a magician who'd just sawed somebody in half. One drink, she told herself. One drink for each of them. Get some food in him. Talk him off the cliff, then send him home. Maybe two drinks—she deserved to cut loose after the hours she'd put in this week. If she got on the ferry by nine, she could be in bed at a halfway decent hour.

As if.

CHAPTER EIGHT

Lussi spent a big chunk of her commuting hours on the Staten Island Ferry. Sometimes she read. Other times she just took in the breeze. If she was feeling feisty, she would wave at the Statue of Liberty like a tourist. This morning, she spent the forty-minute ride across choppy water with her head between her knees. It was only by the grace of God that she didn't get sick on herself.

This was the hangover from hell.

She blamed the devil.

After finally ceding to Fabien's requests for her to partake of the absinthe, the night had dissolved around her. She only remembered bits and pieces from that point, images that made no sense out of context. Topless, muscled men in leather pants. Lussi and Fabien racing a pair of decorative reindeer down an icy sidewalk, laughing in a drunken blur, and then . . . that was all. How she'd made it home last night, she had no idea—an expensive cab that she couldn't afford, no doubt. All she knew was that it was her first and last time drinking absinthe. She hadn't gotten that tanked since freshman year of high school.

At least, unlike poor van Gogh, she'd woken up with both of her ears.

Thank God the Christmas party would take up the whole afternoon.

—

Lussi's office door was open a crack. She'd locked it last night, hadn't she? She gave it a tentative push and was greeted by the sight of a relaxed young man, sitting in her chair, feet propped up on her desk. With his parted blond hair, chunky black glasses, bright yellow polo, and blue loafers, he looked like an illustration from *The Official Preppy Handbook*. Was this the right office? Of course it was. There were her display copies on the bookshelves.

"You must be Lussi," the young man said with unearned confidence. "I'm Cal. The new intern. I was told to report to your office. The door was open, so . . ."

Lussi hung her vintage peacoat on the hook she'd screwed into the drywall. "This isn't a dorm room. Feet off the desk." Cal immediately swung his long legs off the desk and vacated her chair.

"Have you been here long?" she asked, shaking his hand. He had a firm handshake that matched his broad shoulders.

"Only an hour. I've just been reading a book I found on your shelves. I hope that's okay."

Lussi arched a brow. "You know, there's a giant stack of manuscripts right over there," she said, settling in behind her desk. "And there's more where that came from in the basement. Let's get through this pile today and then you can bring more up first thing on Monday. How does—"

He had taken a seat in the chair across from her, and now, unbelievably, his feet were back on the desk. She did not have the patience to house-train a new intern today. She rolled up a manuscript and swatted his shin, which sent him into a yelping fit. "Oh, hush," she said. "It's not like I broke it, though maybe I will if you do it again."

Cal rubbed his shin with a wounded look in his eyes. She glanced at the book he'd been reading. *The Decapitation Chronicles*. Cult movie star Sandy Chainsaw's final, posthumous release. Sandy—real name: Deborah Leavy Morgan—was one of the first authors Lussi had worked with, back when she'd been a lowly editorial assistant at another defunct small publisher.

"How is the book?" Lussi asked Cal. She tried not to think about the grim fate that had befallen the actress. As they say, though: live by the chainsaw, die by the chainsaw.

"It's kind of scary," Cal said.

"That's the idea," she said. "I'm trying to find the next horror superstar. Like Stephen King, but different. A new voice."

He scratched his clean-shaven chin. "Does he have any children?"

"Stephen King?" Lussi said absentmindedly. "Two or three, I think. He doesn't exactly trot them out at conventions."

"Talent is a shared genetic trait," he said. "That's what I've learned at film school, at least. Let's see, you've got Kirk and Michael Douglas. Donald and Kiefer Sutherland. Martin and Charlie Sheen . . ."

"Judy Garland and Liza Minnelli."

Cal's face went blank.

Lussi sighed. Kids these days. "What is it that drew you to publishing?"

"Are you asking if I like books?"

"That *is* what we publish here."

He shrugged. "I was supposed to go home over winter break, but my dad's going to the Bahamas with his new wife. This was the only internship posted on the department board at City College."

Strange that Digby had plucked him from a film program, but it ultimately didn't make much difference to her. As long as he was here to help, he could have been a Reaganomics major for all she cared.

An unpleasant odor drifted past her nose. It was positively vile. "Do you smell something?"

Cal shook his head. "I've got a cold."

And now I'm going to have to disinfect my desk, she thought. Today was *not* the day to come in with a hangover.

"It smells like . . . like a dog's—" Lussi looked down at her feet. The black, polished shoe on her left foot was pressed into a single brown turd the size of a bratwurst. This hadn't been tracked in from outside; she would have noticed that. Had somebody let a dog into her office?

Cal leaned over the desk to get a look at what Lussi had stepped in. "It's not one of mine."

She shot him a blank stare.

"Too small," he explained.

The Blackwood Building was even more gothic than she'd expected, in ways she never could have anticipated. For instance: there were no mirrors above the sinks in the women's restroom. The wall was simply painted black. *Welcome to Castle Dracula.* She had already begun to suspect Mr. Blackwood had been something of a cheapskate, but this bordered on the absurd. How did the women in the office reapply their makeup or fix their hair?

Today, as she scrubbed her shoe clean, she was grateful for the old man's miserliness. At least she didn't have to look at her own hungover reflection. Or her guilty face. She'd really laid into Cal for kicking his feet up on her desk. Oh, well. The sooner he learned that this was a publishing house and not a dorm lounge, the better.

Lussi was running the heel of her shoe under the faucet when the restroom door banged open. It was The Raven. The editor in chief took one look at Lussi's shoe and smirked. "Looks like somebody needs to have a talk with Alan again."

The maintenance man. Lussi hadn't seen him all week, even in passing. He was said to work odd hours. If he cleaned up messes like this, that meant they had him doing double duty as a custodian. Xavier really had been cheap.

The Raven disappeared into the single stall. Lussi imagined the higher-up editors from the big publishers getting together once a month at some swank apartment in Trump Tower overlooking Central Park, trading war stories from the trenches over bacon-wrapped gherkins. *You'll never guess what the new girl stepped in . . .*

Lussi heard the flint of a lighter, followed by a plume of sweet-smelling smoke. Lussi was no stranger to marijuana, but the brazenness of toking up at work—with a coworker around, no less—shocked her. She continued scrubbing.

It wasn't like it was coke. And anyway, who was going to tell The Raven no? She was widely respected and feared in the industry for her intelligence and ruthlessness. She had edited some of the biggest names in literary fiction over the past thirty years. Roth. Plimpton. Cheever. She only worked with male authors—not because she was a misogynist, but because her editing notes were so cutting that they'd reportedly caused a pregnant author to miscarry.

"I'd tell you to call maintenance to clean it up, but it's faster to do it yourself."

"My intern already took care of the mess on the carpet," Lussi said.

There was a long silence. The air was hazy with smoke. "We haven't had an intern around here in some time. Agnes Bailey was in charge of the program. With her gone . . ."

"Mr. Blackwood—the new Mr. Blackwood—hired him, I guess. I'm not even sure if I have him exclusively. Maybe I can lend him out to you, if you need a hand."

An even longer silence followed. "We've never had a genre editor around here either, you know. I never thought I'd live to see the day."

"Well, Mr. Blackwood—the old Mr. Blackwood—interviewed me, and I—"

"Then you saw how the Parkinson's had affected him. It was eating away at his body and his mind. Such a sad, sad ending for such a brilliant man. Painful to watch. That his heart disease took him when it did—well, it was a blessing in disguise. This branch into the supernatural . . . no offense, but it's only more evidence of the severity of his mental decline. And his son, the Boy Blunder . . . well, let's just say the apple doesn't fall far from the tree."

Lussi felt the muscles in her neck tensing. She held her tongue and toweled her shoe dry. "So, whose dog is running around the office? Just in case I step in another you-know-what."

The Raven's reply was drowned by the flushing toilet.

"I'm sorry, I didn't catch that," Lussi said.

The Raven stepped out of the stall. Her eyes were red as Lussi's line-editing pen. "I said," The Raven began, "that it's Alan's."

"What's the breed? I love dogs, but my lease—"

"I didn't say Alan has a dog," The Raven said, slowly enunciating her words. "I said, *it's Alan's*."

It took a moment for what she was saying to sink in. Once it did, Lussi started to laugh. It was probably the pot, but it felt good to let it out. The Raven joined in, and soon they were both laughing so hard that they were coughing (which might have also had something to do with the pot). By the time they settled down, there were tears streaming down Lussi's face. And also, presumably, eyeliner. Good thing she had a compact mirror in her handbag.

The Raven's makeup did not run. Her eyeliner appeared to be tattooed on. Same with her eyebrows and God knew what else.

"You're kidding about Alan," Lussi said. "Right?"

"See you at the party," The Raven said with a thin-lipped smile, leaving Lussi with a contact high and about a million questions.

CHAPTER NINE

"No. Freaking. Way."

Lussi was in the break room, staring into the fridge as if she were gazing into the abyss. The door was open, "letting all the cold air out," as her mother would have put it. Her mother would have understood, though, because an even greater sin had been committed.

Somebody had stolen her stollen.

The Christmas party was scheduled to start in less than an hour. After running out of time to grab her fruitcake for the editorial meeting, Lussi had decided to save it for the office party. She hadn't drawn anyone's name for the exchange, but it felt wrong to go empty-handed—especially since there was a gift waiting for her under the tree. She'd peeked Monday afternoon. The red-and-green striped box with her name on it didn't look threatening. The idea that it was a prank had slowly subsided as the week had worn on. But now . . .

Lussi couldn't imagine someone taking her fruitcake by accident. Trouble was, there were too many suspects. Not even Robert Urich could solve this mystery.

"Mind if I grab my lunch there, chief?" Sloppy Joe said, lumbering into the break room.

She held the fridge door open for him. "You haven't seen a fruitcake around here, have you?" she asked. "It seems to have gotten up and walked away."

"Lose your lunch, eh? I'll tell you what."

"What?"

"Huh?"

"You said, 'I'll tell you—'"

He closed the fridge. "I shouldn't say anything, but . . ." He glanced around nervously. "You know who loved fruitcake?"

She shook her head.

"Mr. Blackwood," he whispered.

She raised an eyebrow. "You think your new boss is a food snatcher."

"Not Digby," he said. He lowered his voice. "Xavier."

"Sorry, I don't think you're understanding me. I put it in the fridge Monday. Mr. Blackwood died *last week*."

As the microwave hummed to life, Sloppy Joe turned to her. "May I inquire about your views on life after death? More to the point . . . do you believe in ghosts?"

She'd long since ruled out any malice in Sloppy Joe's warnings about the basement. How had she suspected this man of orchestrating or participating in a prank of any kind? She felt silly even thinking about it. He was earnest to a fault. That didn't mean she was about to get into a serious metaphysical discussion with him. Especially not in the ninety seconds it took him to heat up his lasagna.

"I've never heard of a ghost that eats fruitcake," Lussi said, sidestepping his question. "In fact, I've never heard of a ghost that eats *anything*. They don't need to eat. They're dead."

"Did you see *Ghostbusters*? I took my grandkids. There was this fat green fella in the movie, ate all the hot dogs." The man snort-laughed, and his jowls wiggled. "Then again, maybe Mr. Black-wood's ghost is just messing with you. I'm not an expert on these things. I thought you might be, because . . ." He let the sentence trail off and stared at her awkwardly.

The microwave dinged.

"You better get that," Lussi said. She turned on her heel, leaving Sloppy Joe to his lunch. "And to whoever stole my fruitcake," she added under her breath, "I hope you have fun choking on it."

CHAPTER TEN

Lussi sipped her punch alone at a fold-out card table in the lobby. She was having flashbacks of family Christmases past, when she'd been exiled with her sister to the kids' table in the den. She hadn't moved up to the adult table until she was fifteen, by which point she already had a learner's permit and her first kiss. Turned out there was more to being an adult than driving and kissing, though. A lot more.

Lussi had a bad habit of arriving at parties too early, but at least she had the opportunity to "appreciate" the lobby's complete transformation. Over the course of the week, a decorations committee had been decking the halls in multicolored garlands, tinsel, and Christmas lights recycled from previous years' holiday displays. If the intention was to make everyone feel like they were suffocating to death with Christmas cheer, then the committee had succeeded.

The food wasn't as substantial as Lussi had hoped for—crackers, cheese, peanut M&M's—but food was never the point of a publishing party. It was all about the alcohol. Whoever had been in charge of making the punch this year had taken a light hand with the vodka. Still, it satisfied the basic requirements of hair of the dog. She took another sip. Her hangover was dissipating, soon to be traded for tomorrow's.

One of her favorite Christmas records, Darlene Love's "Baby Please Come Home," played from a boom box in the corner of the room as the rest of the staff trickled in. You couldn't even tell that the head of the company had just died. Maybe it was what Mr. Blackwood would have wanted? Lussi had a hard time believing that. It was the type of thing you tell yourself when your distant relative dies in a far, faraway land (Florida) but you have tickets to see David Bowie the day of the funeral. Hypothetically.

(Hey, it wasn't like he toured the States that often.)

Lussi looked up hopefully, waiting for one of her colleagues to sit next to her, but everyone naturally gathered in their preset cliques. She had looked for Cal before coming downstairs so she'd have *someone* to talk to, but he was nowhere to be found. Maybe he had gone to lunch and gotten lost on his way back? Interns were unpredictable. They were either try-hards or total duds. She was worried Cal was the latter. He'd talked about *Romancing the Stone* for a solid hour while they sorted through manuscripts together.

"Some party," Digby said, setting his Styrofoam plate down. The stubble was new. Was that a five o'clock shadow, or had he forgotten to shave this morning?

"It's not too bad, as far as office parties go," Lussi said.

He glanced around. "I used to work on Wall Street, you know. Before all this."

"The book industry is, like, the total opposite of the financial industry, I'd bet."

"No kidding. If this was a Wall Street party, there'd be a live DJ . . . an open bar . . . exotic dancers . . ."

"That doesn't sound very Christmas-y."

"It is if the dancers are wearing mistletoe pasties."

She laughed. "Welcome to publishing."

He raised his glass. "And welcome to the new kids' table."

—

Three cups of punch later, Lussi realized just how much vodka was really in it. Digby had gotten up to make the rounds, and she decided to do the same. She approached the friendliest-looking person in the room, an older woman with a hippie vibe.

"Delores in publicity and marketing," the woman shouted over "Like a Virgin." (Clearly whoever was manning the boom box had tired of Christmas music.) Delores was a longtime East Village resident who had been a theater major in college. She still acted when the bug bit her. "My partner just cast me as Death in his off-Broadway production of *Death Takes a Drive in the Country*. He's half my age, a real artist. He's got such a neat aesthetic. Imagine Flannery O'Connor on cough medicine." Lussi nodded, and said she'd like to see that sometime. She enjoyed a good train wreck.

Brian worked in production. He was also a fiddle player. He traveled to Virginia on the weekends to gig with an authentic Civil War–era band. Not a re-creation band, but a band that had been playing together since the Civil War. "There have been a few lineup changes since then," he added.

"Like Kiss," Lussi said.

He nodded. "Actually, we bring a similar energy. Except without all the fire and makeup and groupies." He leaned close to her. She was afraid he was going to put her on the list for one of his shows, but instead he started to gush about *Satan's Lament*. "A little birdie told me you worked on that. I can't believe it. Did you meet Christopher Walken?"

"They don't normally invite editors to film shoots."

"Oh." He shrugged. "Our books never get made into movies."

"Let's see if we can change that," she said. She downed the last of her punch. "If you'll excuse me . . ."

She refilled her drink. It was nice to know not everyone was a literary snob around here. It wouldn't hurt her to let her guard down a little. Her coworkers had probably been standoffish all week since those were the vibes they'd been picking up from her.

A woman with a dozen bracelets on each wrist sidled up next to her at the punch bowl. "Rachael Van Way," the woman said. "Designer." She lived at the Dakota, the building where John Lennon was shot. The gothic apartment complex was where one of Lussi's favorite movies, *Rosemary's Baby*, was filmed. "You should come over sometime!" Rachael shouted over Prince's "Little Red Corvette." "I know the woman who lives in the *Rosemary* apartment. I can totally give you a tour."

"I'll bring my kitchen knife," Lussi said, and Rachael snort-laughed, spilling red punch on the white tablecloth.

Lussi couldn't keep track of every face and name, but one thing was for sure: her new coworkers were quirkier than she'd given them credit for. They weren't just a bunch of stuffed shirts. She was even starting to like them a little bit. She'd let go of her anger over the missing fruitcake. Someone got hungry. That was all. Forgive and forget. Oma's words. Lussi settled into a pleasant buzz. For the first time all week, she felt like she was starting to fit in. Everything looked like it might come together after all. And then The Raven had to go and ruin it all.

"Turn down the music and take a seat, everyone," The Raven shouted. "It's time for Secret Santa."

CHAPTER ELEVEN

Lussi's stomach clenched as she returned to the new kids' table. Digby was already seated. She'd almost forgotten about the gift exchange.

"As you know, everyone was assigned a colleague to buy a gift for and told not to spend more than twenty-five dollars. We'll open gifts one at a time, and each person will guess who bought their gift for them. There's no extra reward for guessing correctly, but as we know, bragging rights are everything in publishing." Everyone chuckled appreciatively—even Lussi.

Dracula's Brides—whom Lussi still couldn't identify by name—gathered the gifts from under the tree and began to hand them out. Bride #1 set a small box wrapped in bright red paper in front of Digby. It looked like somebody had used an entire roll of Scotch tape on it. Digby turned his gift over, then held it to his ear. He gave it a quick shake.

"Stop that," Lussi said, reaching for the box before she realized what she was doing.

"Is there something breakable in here?" Digby asked, holding it out of Lussi's reach. "If it's from you, just tell me."

"It's supposed to be anonymous," Lussi said.

"So is AA, but the first thing you do there is introduce your-self."

"I'll take your word for it," she said. "But, no, it's not from me. I just think it's bad luck to shake presents. My mother told me that if you shook a present, it would change from something you wanted into a sweater. I never believed her, of course. But I never shook a present after that, either."

"I wouldn't mind a sweater," Digby said, gleefully shaking the package with both hands. The box wasn't large enough for a sweater. Maybe a sweater for a tiny dog, like the kind she saw the women near Grammercy Park carrying in their handbags.

Bride #2 dropped Lussi's gift on the card table, the same box that had been sitting under the tree all week. Since the cardboard was printed with a striped holiday pattern, her Secret Santa hadn't bothered wrapping it. The lid was held in place with a ribbon. The handwriting on the tag was finely printed. FOR: LUSSI. On the flipside, FROM: SANTA.

"Does everyone have a gift?" The Raven asked. Lussi scanned the room nervously, on the off chance that her Secret Santa had left someone else out on her account. Everyone had a gift, though.

"As is customary, we'll start with our most tenured members and work our way to the virgins." The Raven cast a cold look at Digby, as if to say, *That would be you, you worthless corporate suit*, and then let her glance travel to Lussi. *And you, the editor who's on a mission to destroy the legacy of this illustrious company.*

—

Though the company was fairly small, it took about an hour to get to Lussi between all the *ooh*ing and *ahh*ing and the guessing, which seemed to be the real fun for most people. Most of the presents were gag gifts that obviously spoke to some inside joke between the gifter and giftee. Delores cried when she unwrapped her rubber chicken, which was met with delighted applause. Brian was clearly touched by a sock full of $25 in quarters. Rachael couldn't stop laughing at the can of Campbell's tomato soup and the potato she received.

Digby's present turned out not to be a sweater but a plastic bendable Gumby from Maureen, an ancient production editor. Digby looked up, amazed. "It's just like the one I used to play with in the office when I was a boy."

"It's not *just* like it—it *is* it. I nicked it from you because you kept throwing it at my face," Maureen said. Everyone laughed as Digby stared wondrously at the toy.

"Last but not least, Ms. Meyer," The Raven said, a chill in her tone.

Lussi felt a lump growing in her throat. She'd been keeping track of who gifted what to whom. Every "Santa" had been accounted for. Suddenly, all the worry about it being a prank returned.

She removed the fat red bow and then carefully undid the ribbon. She paused with her hand on the lid. The room was silent; the tape had reached the end of Side A long ago, and nobody had flipped it.

Lussi lifted the lid. She gasped audibly.

It was the Percht from Mr. Blackwood's office. It wasn't in the best shape. Antiques never are. The torso would need to be replaced, obviously, as the animal pelt was mottled and peeling away. The paint needed to be stripped and reapplied to the wooden head. This could be a fun repair project. She felt charged up, raring to go. A warm feeling flooded her every sense, and—

"What is that thing?" Digby whispered, leaning over to peek in the box. His face was scrunched up in confusion.

She snapped back to focus. She'd been lost there for a moment. Her coworkers, at first silent, were now whispering amongst themselves. They were waiting for her to take her gift out and show it off.

"You don't recognize it?" she asked Digby. He was the only one who could have given it to her. The only one with access to his father's things.

He shook his head.

Lussi was stumped. It wasn't a gift from Xavier Blackwood. That much she knew. No matter what Sloppy Joe said, Mr. Blackwood's ghost was not haunting the building for the sole purpose of making her life difficult. Or for passing on his earthly possessions. The alternatives, though, were equally unpleasant: either the Percht was stolen from Mr. Blackwood's office, or someone had pilfered it from the trash after his office was cleaned out.

The chatter in the room had quieted down. People wanted answers. "Come on, get on with it," someone said. "The booze ain't gonna drink itself."

Lussi's jaw tightened. This was precisely what she'd been worried about when she'd heard she had a gift under the tree. One of her coworkers had thought the Percht looked weird and creepy. They thought *she* was weird and creepy. It was only an accident of fate that she even knew what it was. *Well, you know what?* she thought. *I'm not giving whoever did this the satisfaction.*

She set the lid back on the box. "It's empty," she said, ignoring Digby's questioning look. "An empty box. So, thanks, Santa. Next year, how about some coal at least?"

A few awkward laughs. A lot of confusion. Commence the binge drinking.

High school all over again.

Now she just had to find the bully.

CHAPTER TWELVE

The party resumed. Digby sat in silence with her for a few minutes, and then made some strained excuse to leave their table. "The boss is expected to mingle," he said with a laugh. He didn't ask her why she'd lied about what was in the box. If he was even the least bit curious, he didn't show it.

She watched him go straight to the men's room.

And just like that, she was back to being an outsider.

Lussi slipped quietly upstairs with her gift box. In her office, she removed the doll. If there was any truth to Oma's tales about the Perchten warding off evil, maybe this little guy would do her some good. Maybe it could do a number on whoever was making her life here difficult. "You'll help me out, won't you, Perky?" she said, picking him up. This wasn't the Perky from her childhood, but she was one of those weirdos who recycled pet names.

She'd had seven gerbils, all named Harold.

"I guess we're both a little strange," she said, giving Perky's fur-covered body a squeeze. The doll's insides crunched underneath the animal pelt. Whatever it was filled with had gone rotten. Her mind conjured images of broken eggshells, fishbones. Dried beetles. A slideshow of gruesome images popped into her head.

She let out a sharp shriek and dropped the doll.

Perky laid on the carpet, motionless. She picked it up and gave it a quick poke, right in its belly. No crunch. No strange sensations. She squeezed it. It was filled with cotton, or whatever stuffing went inside kids' toys.

She'd read one too many lousy horror manuscripts this week. That was all. The relentless parade of unnecessary adverbs had begun to infect her. That, plus she had a slight buzz.

She set the doll on her bookshelf. Time to call it a night.

There was a knock at her door. She didn't want to talk to anyone. She just wanted to slip out, unnoticed. "I'm not in here," she said.

The door opened a crack, and a massively coiffed head popped through. Fabien Nightingale. What was he doing here? She waved him in and told him to close the door. He was bundled up in his fur coat and striped scarf, with a pair of oversized Elton John shades. He looked like a gay character in a Dickens novel. Or a Dickens character in a gay novel.

Without taking off his shades or jacket, Fabien slid into the open chair across from her desk. "This place isn't as creepy as I'd expected," he said. "It's worse. It smells like . . ."

"A dog park?"

"A nursing home."

He wasn't wrong, but she had no idea how he could smell anything aside from his cologne. Lussi rubbed her eyes. He must have laid it on thicker than usual to cover the absinthe seeping from his pores.

"You all right, love?" Fabien asked. "Why aren't you downstairs?"

"Still nursing that hangover from last night," she fibbed. He hadn't come to listen to her complain about office politics. Actually, what *was* he doing here? She was surprised he'd been let into the building in the first place, and even more surprised someone had apparently shown him to her office. Authors didn't usually drop by their publishers' offices unannounced. At least the sane ones didn't. "Were you in the neighborhood today, or . . ."

"You invited me," he said. "You told me to bring a little *fée verte* to spike the punch and said we could entertain ourselves by making bets on who was going to hook up. I've brought plenty of ones and fives."

"I did not say that." She shook her head. "Did I?"

He picked up a manuscript from her desk. "You did indeed," he said, reading over the query letter. "Perhaps you'd better leave the drinking to the professionals. Your liver will thank you later." He turned the page. "'Last Thursday night was the first time I saw the werewolf pissing on my grandmother's grave.' This sounds promising."

"You'd think so, right? It's all downhill from there."

He flipped through a few more pages before tossing it onto her desk. "I'll take your word for it. Anyway, brought you a present," he said, reaching into his jacket's inner recesses.

"If it's absinthe—"

"Don't worry, I already emptied my flask into the punch downstairs."

Lussi buried her head in her hands.

"What? A punch bowl at a holiday party is asking to be spiked," he said.

"That punch was already spiked."

He raised a brow. "Well, it's Christmas."

"What's that supposed to mean?"

"That is none of your business and certainly none of mine." He pulled out a rolled-up manuscript and flattened it as best as he could on the edge of the desk. "Here's the reason I transferred on the subway *twice* from the Upper West Side."

She read the title out loud: "*Transylvanian Dirt*."

"You said last night you wanted to read it. Though I'm beginning to understand you may not have been in full control of your faculties . . ."

She scanned the first few pages. A prologue set in Nazi Germany. That would have to go. She flipped through the manuscript, reading a line here and there.

Fabien added, "I've been saying this for a while, but vampires are going to come back in a big, big way. You can get ahead of the curve with this."

"Wait, this is a vampire novel? They're dead, Fabien."

"You mean *undead*."

She groaned. Bloodsuckers came and went in cycles, like cicada broods. Anne Rice had breathed fresh life into the monsters a decade ago with *Interview with the Vampire* (a formative book for teenage Lussi), and a biblical flood of vampire novels followed. A few were notable: *A Delicate Dependency. The Vampire Tapestry.* But only a few. Most should have had stakes driven through them. Readers had soured on vampires in recent years due to the glut.

Fabien wasn't having it. "I've been out there. Among the people. In Wichita. In Toledo. I see what they read. That book by those splatterpunk knobs has sold over half a million copies. Go tell them vampires are old hat."

The Light at the End was a bonanza of blood and tits, written by a pair of failed rock musicians. It crossed lines of good taste Lussi had previously been oblivious to. It was many things, but a sign that vampires were on the upswing wasn't one of them.

"Refresh my memory," Lussi said. "Have you showed any of this to your editor at Harper yet?"

"Do you think I would be here if I hadn't?"

Lussi raised an eyebrow.

"Rest easy," he said. "It was a 'thanks, but no thanks' from the good folks at your former employer."

"I never got the chance to work for them. They laid me off."

"A mere technicality. Much like an option."

"Fabien, I swear, if you haven't cleared this with them . . ."

He waved a hand dismissively. "I've got the rejection letter at home. Suitable for framing. Could you just read this thing? It's either the best thing I've ever done or the worst. I'm not asking you to publish it. You're not my editor anymore, but you're the only person in this decrepit industry whose opinion I care about. My agent wants to send it wide next week. I just need to know I'm not embarrassing myself here."

She didn't see how she could fit it into her schedule, with all she had to do by the end of the year. But she also didn't see how she could tell him no.

"I'll take a look this weekend," she said.

He didn't thank her. Instead, he was staring past her. "Where did you get that?"

She followed his gaze to the doll on her bookshelf. She'd positioned it as a bookend to her small collection of Broken Angel best sellers.

"It's a Secret Santa gift," she said. "A Percht. Some weird German doll. It used to belong to Mr. Blackwood. It's like a dream catcher—it's supposed to keep evil spirits at bay."

Fabien walked around her desk. Picked it up. "Do you know its age?"

"I'm assuming it's old. Xavier Blackwood was old. Old people like old things."

"Your powers of deductive reasoning never fail to astonish me,"

Fabien said with a smile. He set the doll back on the shelf. "You said it was a Percht? Is that any relation to Frau Perchta?"

"I wouldn't know," Lussi said. For all the warm feelings she had for her grandmother, she remembered precious little of her stories. Which was for the best, her sister would have said.

Fabien didn't say anything. He turned to the window. The blinds were up. The park across the street was alive with fire and energy tonight. Dusk was when neighborhoods showed their true selves. Was it Nelson Algren who'd said that? Some American poet.

Fabien placed a finger on the glass and traced the length of one of the black bars. "Iron is often used to keep evil spirits at bay as well, you know," he said. "What do you suppose the old man was afraid of?"

CHAPTER THIRTEEN

After she saw Fabien out, Lussi returned to her office. The party was still raging downstairs, but no one had paid her attention as she'd cut through the lobby. She slipped his manuscript into her work bag. She also noticed a tote bag resting on the floor beside her desk. Was it Fabien's, or . . . ? Lussi peered into the bag and saw the Sandy Chainsaw novel Cal had been reading earlier. *Cal's still here?* She'd assumed he'd left when she couldn't find him before the party.

But there was one place she hadn't thought to look. The place where he was most likely to be.

The basement.

She vaguely remembered telling him that she wanted him to get more manuscripts for her on Monday morning. Maybe he was a try-hard after all and had gone down that afternoon? Lussi felt her chest tighten, remembering how she'd been trapped in the dark steel cage. If Cal was stuck in there, no one would be able to hear him over the loud music—especially now that everyone was plastered.

She pulled open the top drawer of her desk and retrieved the flashlight she'd picked up at a hardware store after her little episode in the basement.

As she made her way down the spiral staircase, she noticed the crowd was starting to thin. She made it to the basement door without anyone stopping her. She pulled the chain at the top of the staircase.

Nothing. Now this bulb was out, too? Great.

"Cal, I swear to God, you better be down here," she muttered. She switched on the flashlight and called out for Cal. She waited for a reply. No response. She descended the stairs and cast the beam around. The metal cage with the slush pile was beyond the flashlight's range. "Cal?" she said again.

He wasn't down here. She would have heard him rattling the door if he'd been trapped. And anyway, a strong, sturdy young man like Cal could have ripped the door off its hinges. He might have dressed like Clark Kent, but he was built like Superman. She started back up the stairs when she heard a low mewling sound.

She carefully lowered herself in a crouching position, shining the beam around. "Is someone down here?"

The mewling continued; it sounded more animal than human. A wounded or starving animal. She tried the downstairs lights, but they weren't working. She took slow, steady steps so as not to clack her chunky heels against the concrete. If it was a cat in need of medical attention, she didn't want to scare it into hiding.

A gray blur shot across the floor in the path of her flashlight. She tried to follow it with the beam, but all she caught was a thin pink tail disappearing under the shelving. People back home always asked her if the subway rats were really "as big as they say on the TV." *No*, she would tell them. *They're bigger.*

The mewling had stopped. She whistled, hoping to draw the

cat out. Sometimes that worked with Radcliffe, her eight-year-old tabby. Sometimes it didn't work, of course. Cats are gonna cat.

Her whistling morphed into the opening theme to *The Andy Griffith Show*. Lussi had always found Mayberry disturbing. It wasn't a small town—it was a black-and-white purgatory, a spiritual pit stop on the road to heaven. Andy, Opie, Aunt Bee . . . all trapped in Mayberry, repeating the same mistakes over and over, until their sins were fully cleansed. Lussi was four when she'd developed this theory. Her parents stopped taking her to CCD after that.

Lussi quit whistling . . . but the *Andy Griffith* theme continued.

Unless there was a whistling cat in the building, someone was down here after all.

——

Lussi froze. She could hear sobs mixed in between bars of the song. It hadn't been a cat that she'd heard. It had been a person.

A person crying.

"Cal?" she said, creeping toward the whistling. She rounded the corner and found the whistler leaning against a stack of boxes, surrounded by a mess of papers. Digby. Drunk out of his mind, from the sound of it.

He covered his eyes to see past the flashlight. "Dad? You came back for one last laugh, eh. Go ahead, then. Laugh. Get it out of your system, you . . . you miserable old . . . old . . ."

Lussi turned the light around, illuminating her face. "It's me. Lussi."

He laughed. It sounded like he was out of his mind. "Check out what Secret Santa brought me," he said, showing off the little plastic toy. "Maureen had it the whole time."

Lussi sat cross-legged next to him. An empty bottle of Jack Daniel's was tipped over beside him. Was it possible to drink so much whiskey that you could speak with your dead father? A question for another time, perhaps.

"The lights cut out again," he said. "When I find Alan, I'm going to . . ." His voice trailed off. "Look at this."

He held up a green-and-white-striped computer printout. She directed the flashlight at it but it was only a blur of numbers to her. The last math class she'd taken was in high school.

"An old balance sheet," he said by way of explanation. "Not only is this company in the red this year, but it appears it's never turned a profit. Ever. If the old man had some sort of shadow investor who kept it propped up all these years, he never told me. Or recorded it in the books."

Lussi hadn't been a business major, but even she knew you couldn't lose money every year for forty years and still churn out books. Digby had to be misreading the reports. Could he even see straight right now? He was in no shape to analyze his own health, let alone the company's.

"I can hear my father's voice, still. In these walls. He's not done with me." Digby shook his head. "But I'm done with him. This company . . . this building. It's all one big joke. That's the only reason he willed it to me, and not to his little tramp, Agnes."

"His secretary? Isn't she, like, ninety?"

"She looks it. I have no idea of her actual age. When my father first started sleeping with her, he was still married to my mother. The divorce dragged on for years and years. My childhood was a procession of court dates. He never remarried, but I got the impression he was still carrying on with Agnes. I would have fired her after I settled in, and I would have enjoyed it."

"You didn't fire her."

"The last time I saw her was at the hospital, the day my father bit the big one. She called in the next day to tell Gail she quit. Didn't even return to clear out her desk."

"Sounds like she knew what you were planning."

"She knew before I did. Nobody quits this company—that's what Dad used to say. Well, somebody finally did. She deserves every terrible thing that life is going to throw at her, now that she's alone and unemployed." He paused. "I'm sorry. My emotions . . . That's too far. I shouldn't say such awful things. Especially about old ladies."

He picked up his bottle, saw it was empty, and heaved it at the far wall. It shattered on impact, raining glass shards onto the floor. Lussi bit her lip. She didn't know why Digby was opening up to her. She guessed that—like most men—he was simply looking for an audience, and she was the closest thing.

His head wobbled, threatening to fall right off his neck. How he'd made it down here without landing on his face, she didn't know. But he was in no condition to go back. She decided to leave him the flashlight. It was past time for her to go home for the day. Cal had probably left his tote bag in her office on purpose and was bar-hopping his way through St. Marks with his friends.

"Why don't we let you sleep it off down here, okay?"

His eyes were already closed, and he was snoring loudly. She pointed the flashlight in the direction of the stairs. A straight shot. She turned it off and was about to put it in Digby's hands when the mewling started up again. It wasn't Digby. It was coming from behind her.

Lussi shined the flashlight back toward the wire cages. The wounded sound was coming from the slush pile. She approached cautiously. She didn't like how pained the mewling sounded . . . and she didn't like where it was coming from. The light was bouncing around, her hand trembling. The closer she got, the wider the area it illuminated. The wire door was open. The towers of manuscripts had toppled, causing tens of thousands of loose papers to spill from the cage . . . and sticking out from underneath them was a single blue loafer.

CHAPTER FOURTEEN

Lussi spent the rest of her Friday night with Cal in the ER.
Diagnosis: fractured tibia, bruised ribs, concussion. Cal had no
memory of the accident, but he'd been lying there in pain for
hours, unable to move under the weight of the slush pile. There
wasn't enough brain bleach in the world to cleanse her mind's eye
of the image of his white shinbone poking through the skin.

"I'm sorry you got hurt on your first day, Cal," she said, holding
his hand until his parents arrived. "I shouldn't have asked you to
get the manuscripts when I knew the basement was in such bad
shape."

"Tha's okay," Cal said through a haze of sedatives. "I's not your
fault. Coulda . . . coulda happened to anyone."

But was that true? Lussi had been down in that basement twice
now. Both times, something strange had happened. What happened
to Cal went beyond hazing—well beyond. Thankfully, all signs
pointed to it being an accident. She sure as hell didn't believe in
ghosts, but something weird was happening in that basement.

Lussi had planned to come in on the weekend to catch up on
submissions. Not now. She needed a break from the building. She
also needed to seriously think about whether she should go back

on Monday. Maybe Blackwood-Patterson wasn't the place for her after all. Money and cool-ass gothic building be damned.

By the time Monday morning rolled around, however, Lussi found herself getting up, getting dressed, and boarding the ferry. She emerged from the subway onto the streets of the East Village an hour later. She couldn't give up so soon. Once more into the fray.

A light snow was falling. First of the season. The side-walks were a wet, slushy mess. The temperature was hovering right around freezing, where it would stay all day, according to Spencer Christian. Lussi hugged her handbag tight as she navigated the rush-hour pedestrian traffic. She was running a few minutes late. Whenever she was behind, it seemed like she was the only one walking with any sense of purpose.

Half the buildings along her two-block route were boarded up with graffiti-covered plywood. It was a tiny detail Lussi had missed the Monday she'd interviewed with Mr. Blackwood. When she was on a mission, she could be dangerously oblivious to the outside world. Someday, she was going to make the front page of the *Post* for falling into an open manhole and getting eaten by a sewer gator.

A towering Black man in a fedora and wool trench coat stepped out from behind a stoop as she passed by. He jogged to catch up to her. "Ms. Meyer? Excuse me, Ms. Meyer?"

Something about him was familiar. Lussi slowed. "Sorry, do I know you?"

"Peter Faber," he said, holding up an open wallet, showing off a brass badge. She stopped to look at it. She only got a quick peek before he snapped his wallet closed. "OSHA inspector. I was hoping we could chat."

He certainly sounded the part of authority, though he didn't look much older than her. "OSHA? Like the posters-in-break-rooms OSHA?"

"That's us," he said with a deep laugh. "Occupational Safety and Health Administration. It's a little cold out here, though. Why don't you let me buy you a coffee? There's a Greek diner just around the corner—"

"If this is about Cal, you'll need to speak with my boss. I'm just an editor." She paused. "*Senior* editor. Now, if you'll excuse me . . ."

"Cal?" he asked, blocking her again as she tried to round him. "Who's Cal?"

She ran her tongue over her front teeth. She could feel something stuck there, a piece of oatmeal from breakfast. "I'm sorry, what's this about again?"

"Every workplace injury is required, by law, to be filed with OSHA. Employers must notify OSHA when an employee is hospitalized or killed on the job. Also, when there's an accidental amputation or optectomy."

"Opt . . ."

He pointed one gloved finger to his eye.

"Oh," she said.

"There's been a string of accidents at Blackwood-Patterson," Peter said. "We have documents dating back to the early seventies. Possibly, what's been happening dates back earlier—that's just when filing requirements were put into place. What we have on file, though, has raised some eyebrows around the office."

She realized where she'd seen him before. Across the street, in Tompkins Square Park last week. Watching her. Or was she imagining that? Two-way traffic passed them on Avenue A at breakneck speed. She'd about had enough of his questions.

"I'm afraid I only started last week," she told him. "I don't see how I could help you with old reports. My boss just started, too—there was some . . . turnover at the top."

"Xavier Blackwood. Heart attack. I read the obit in the *Times*."

"His secretary is gone, too. Quit last week. I'm sure somebody at the office would be able to help you, though. If you want to follow me . . ."

He looked her in the eyes. His gaze was colder than the winter wind. "There's a reason I didn't want to meet at your office. I didn't wait out here for the past hour to ask for your help," he said. He handed her a business card. "I'm here to warn you. I believe your life may be in danger."

━

Lussi slipped through the great iron doorway and shut the door with all her weight. Her breathing was heavy. A lump had formed in her throat, and she couldn't get rid of it. She badly needed something to drink.

"Everything okay, Lussi?" Gail asked.

Life was beginning to return to Lussi's frozen cheeks. After the OSHA inspector had told her to be careful, she'd run toward the building. Mr. Blackwood died of a heart attack. Perfectly natural—she'd witnessed it herself. Even Cal's injuries weren't suspicious. She didn't know what other incidents had occurred over the years, but the workforce was old. The building was old. Fabien had been right when he'd called it a nursing home.

"There was a man . . ." Lussi's voice trailed off. She pulled the business card from her pocket. It wasn't Peter's—this was for a religion editor at Random House. She turned her pockets inside out, but all she found was an old movie ticket stub. Must have dropped the man's card. "It was nothing. Probably."

From underneath her desk, Gail pulled out an impossibly large handgun. It gleamed silver, with black accents. It was the length of Lussi's forearm and as thick as her wrist. A scope was mounted on a top rail.

"I keep this holstered underneath here," Gail said, setting it on her desk to let Lussi have a look at it. "A .357 Magnum, semi-automatic pistol with a nine-round capacity. Telescopic sight with red-dot optics. They call it the Desert Eagle."

"It's not for deer hunting, I take it."

"Heavens, no. There wouldn't be anything left to mount on your wall."

Lussi started for the stairs, then paused. "Do I need to fill out any paperwork for Cal's injury? At my last job, if there was an injury . . ."

Gail was busy wiping down her gun with a rag. "An OSHA report needs to be filed within twenty-four hours. I faxed it over Saturday morning. Nothing you need to worry about."

"You're sure?"

Gail trained her gun at the Christmas tree, squinting to see through the scope. "Trust me, it's all routine. You need to understand, this is an old building. Accidents happen. Nothing too serious. We're covered by insurance."

"What about Frederick?"

An eardrum-bursting thunderclap rocked the building. Lussi shrieked—or at least she thought she did; all she could hear was the ringing in her ears. The glass angel tree-topper lay in glittering pieces on the floor of the lobby. The bullet had practically turned it back into sand.

"Do we need to report that?" Lussi asked. Her voice sounded

distant, underwater.

"N-no," Gail said, the Desert Eagle shaking in her hands. "I'll cl-clean it up."

Several of the staff had rushed to the balustrade in the interim. They were already beginning to file back to their offices, apparently having lost interest once they'd seen nobody had been grievously wounded. Suddenly, Lussi didn't feel quite so safe inside the Blackwood Building. She wasn't sure she was safe outside, either. If this Peter Faber was really an OSHA inspector, wouldn't he have known about Cal's accident? *Unless Gail didn't file it,* Lussi thought to herself as she walked up the spiral staircase to her office. She looked at the iron bars on the windows. For the first time, she wondered who the iron bars were really there to protect. Were the barbarians outside the gates, or inside?

CHAPTER FIFTEEN

For the second workday in a row, Lussi's door was already open upon her arrival. And, as on Friday morning, there was a man sitting in her chair. At least this time there were no feet on her desk.

"I suppose you'll be wanting your chair back," Digby said, taking his headphones off. He'd been listening to a Walkman at full blast. She'd let someone else tell him about the accidental discharge in the lobby.

"Sorry I'm late," she said. She was about to launch into an excuse, but her new boss had a keen eye for bullshit. He also didn't seem to care. "Did we have a meeting scheduled?" she asked.

"No, no. Don't worry, I was just keeping your chair warm for you," he said, jumping to his feet. He caught her staring down at his Gold Toe socks. "Oh, that. I stepped in something in my office. Your intern is off cleaning my shoes. He should be back soon."

"You found me another intern already?"

"Same one," he said. "I wasn't going to clean my own shoes. Not when we have someone paid to do it. Or not paid, as is the case."

"Wait, what's Cal doing here? I assumed he'd never want to

come back."

Digby chuckled. "What can I say? The kid's a trooper. He's hobbling around somewhere on crutches as we speak."

Lussi shook her head. "He told me the other night he's a film major. Doesn't even want to work in publishing. At least he's got moxie."

"No one wants to be in publishing, darling. Yet here we are," Digby said, gesturing around grandly.

Lussi let the comment go. "I stepped in something on Friday, too."

He met her eyes, and she could tell they were both talking about the same type of *something*. "You should have told someone," he said. "Don't worry, though. I've got an exterminator coming tomorrow to take care of the problem."

"An exterminator?"

"If there's a more humane way to handle her, I'll look into it."

Lussi set her handbag down on her desk. "I'm sorry, did you say *her*?"

"Cyndi Lauper." When she didn't respond, he added, "The raccoon. The one that's been running loose in the building."

Damn The Raven. Why had Lussi believed her when she said it was Alan?

Digby went to the window and stared toward the park. "I never got to thank you for taking charge of that whole situation on Friday night, by the way. I'm afraid I wasn't much help. I can usually handle my liquor, but that punch . . . whoa, baby."

Lussi gently cursed Fabien in her mind. Of course that was why he was hallucinating his father's ghost. The little green fairy had gotten to him.

There was a six-inch stack of envelopes on her desk. "It was nothing, really," she said absently, shuffling through the pile. They were all addressed to the submissions editor. The mailroom was now rerouting the slush to her instead of hauling it to the basement.

"Nothing?" he said, turning. "You also helped my father. For what it's worth."

"Right place at the right time. That's all."

"Speaking of my father, his funeral is scheduled for tomorrow. It took forever to find a venue with enough seats."

"Madison Square Garden?" she said, joking.

"Carnegie Hall."

She laughed, but he wasn't smiling. "You're serious."

"As a heart attack." Digby picked up a book off her shelf, flipped through it. "Bad choice of words. He left behind money earmarked for his funeral, but no trust fund. How's the search for the next Stephen King going?"

It was December 15. She'd been on the job for exactly one week, but the month was already almost halfway over. So far, she hadn't found a single publishable novel, let alone one with the potential to turn around an entire company's financial outlook.

Before she could reply, Cal clambered into the office, limping on crutches. A cast covered his shin and his ankle. He said hello to Lussi and handed Digby his loafers. They were polished and did not smell like excrement. Digby slipped them on and told Lussi he'd catch up with her later.

Lussi cast an eye over her bookshelf as she shrugged off her coat. Something didn't look right, and it took her a few moments to realize why: Perky was missing. First her fruitcake, now Mr. Blackwood's doll. Did she have to start writing her name on her stuff with a Sharpie, like her mother had when Lussi was in grade school?

Cal carefully lowered himself into the chair across from Lussi's.

He leaned his crutches against her desk. At least he wouldn't be putting his feet up there anymore.

"Thank you for staying with me on Friday," Cal said.

"Thank you for coming back," Lussi said, smiling warmly at him. "Say, when you came in, did you see a doll about yea tall on my shelf this morning?" she asked, holding her hands a little less than a foot apart.

"A doll? Like Strawberry Shortcake?"

"Not quite. It's got horns and teeth and—"

"I think I'd remember that," he said, "even with all the pain-killers I'm on."

Lussi wondered who else had been in her office. Alan, emptying the trash over the weekend? That theory went out the window when she noticed her wastebasket was still full. She would worry about it later.

She handed Cal a thick stack of manuscripts. "Get comfy. You can sit here and read all day. I'll get you trained on the phone tomorrow."

There was a knock at the door. Cal reached for his crutches but Lussi waved him off. "Come in," she shouted.

The Raven craned her head through the door. "Would you mind if I borrowed this young gentleman for a bit?" She gave Lussi a crooked smile. "I'll try not to break his other leg."

Cal's brow furrowed in confusion, trepidation, or some com-bination of both. He looked to Lussi to save him, but she would be of no help. She'd already promised the editor in chief that she'd lend him out. What sort of labor The Raven had in mind for a one-legged twenty-one-year-old, Lussi didn't know.

"Absolutely, Mary Beth. I'll send him over in a minute."

The Raven nodded curtly and left.

Lussi gave Cal a stern look. "If anything weird happens, or if you need to take a moment for yourself, don't hesitate to speak up. Everyone seems to think it's normal for you to break your leg on a Friday and show up on a Monday, but I don't. This is above and beyond—and I don't want you to get hurt again."

Cal tucked his crutches under his arms. "Don't worry, boss. I'm just going down the hall. What could happen?"

Later—after all was said and done—she wished she could have gone back and told him to run from the Blackwood Building, broken leg and all.

CHAPTER SIXTEEN

After lunch, Lussi ventured into the basement to assess the status of the slush pile. She had no interest in sorting things back into stacks—not by herself, at least. Not without someone to spot her in case the towers came crashing down again. At the same time, she couldn't just leave the manuscripts all over the floor. That wasn't how she'd been raised.

Except someone had already taken the initiative. The papers spilling out of the cage had been rounded up. Everything had been restacked, same as before the accident. Not only that, the manuscripts were rubber-banded and paper-clipped together. The only sign that anything untoward had happened down here on Friday were the brick-red stains on the cement floor.

Good enough for her. She turned to leave, and kicked something with the heel of her shoe. Perky. Strange—it hadn't been there a moment ago, she could have sworn. She picked it up. Had she brought it down here Friday night when she'd gone looking for Cal? Not that she could recall. She hadn't drunk that much—certainly nothing like when she'd ripped up the town with Fabien. That unsettling feeling that had begun last Monday returned full force. Somebody—or several somebodies—were trying to mess with her head. She hoped they were having a good laugh at her expense. Because she was going to have the last laugh when she singlehandedly turned this company around.

——

Lussi stopped in the break room for another coffee on her way back up to her office. In just a week, she had tripled her caffeine intake. She couldn't seem to stay awake unless she was in the direct sun, which only filtered into her office in the mornings. A third of the building's bulbs were burned out; the rest might as well have been, for all the good they did. The only overhead lighting was in the basement. The halls and offices were lit with wall sconces, which threw shadows across the walls. On sunny days—like the day of her interview—sunlight flooded the building. On overcast days—and when night settled in—the Blackwood Building seemed to sag under the weight of its gloomy interior. The only way to fight back the darkness was with coffee—black coffee.

Lussi had to brew a new pot. While she waited, she set the doll on the counter and checked out the message board. Somebody had pinned up Xavier Blackwood's *Times* obituary. According to the paper of record, his "long-term personal secretary" had found him slumped in his worn leather chair, a red felt-tip clutched in his frozen left hand.

> Paramedics on the scene confirmed that Mr.
> Blackwood was at work on the next Pulitzer
> Prize—winning novel from the famously high-

brow independent publishing house that he
founded and chaired for nearly forty years ...

She rolled her eyes. She'd learned over the past week that it
had been years since anybody had seen the old man so much as
touch a manuscript. The obit also mentioned that he was a veteran
who had "seen action in the European theater during World War
II." Xavier had been critically wounded, and it was during his
long convalescence that he first fell in love with books. More than
122 million paperbacks had been shipped overseas for servicemen.
When Xavier returned to the United States, he had used family
money to found Blackwood Books.

Left out was the curious fact that it had never turned a profit in
its nearly forty-year existence. *Alleged* fact, Lussi reminded herself.

An arctic draft blew through the break room, followed by a
metallic clanking in the hallway. Lussi went into the hall. The
door to the fire escape was swinging open, banging against the
doorframe every time the wind blew it closed. She'd seen a few
coworkers sneak out the fire escape doors to smoke. It was the only
place she'd worked in that frowned upon indoor smoking—something about the building being a tinderbox. The Raven, of course,
played by her own set of rules.

Lussi poked her head out the door. Whoever had been out here
smoking was long gone, the only evidence a rusted Folgers can full
of butts. A kitchen worker across the alley propped a door open.
He disappeared back into the dim sum restaurant, then returned
with a sack of trash that he heaved into the dumpster. How did
he get by in this city? Easy, she thought: he wasn't in publishing. It
was rumored that the food service industry paid its workers living
wages. Of course, she'd also heard that restaurants exploited their

workers, many of whom were undocumented aliens. What right did she have to complain?

The wind picked up. She was about to pull the door closed when she noticed she could see straight into the conference room from the platform. The blinds were angled in such a way that she had a clear view inside . . . and what she saw confused her. The entire editorial team was seated at the table, along with Cal. The sales team (all two of them) were there. Stanley. Gail. She couldn't see the entire room from her vantage point, but it sure looked like an all-hands-on-deck meeting. All hands except for Lussi.

One thing was for sure: they weren't planning her a surprise birthday party.

Her birthday was in July.

Maybe Gail had circulated a memo about the meeting and it was buried under the stack of mail on Lussi's desk. Maybe The Raven had mentioned it in one of the meetings last week, and she'd just forgotten to put it in her day planner. Meetings, meetings, meetings—that's all they seemed to do at Blackwood-Patterson. In that respect, the company wasn't much different from every other publishing house in Manhattan. The average publishing workday was a blur of production meetings, sales meetings, cover design meetings . . . and, Lussi's favorite, meetings to schedule future meetings.

She had no clue what the all-hands was about. It could have been a meeting to discuss the summer catalog, or that they were switching the Coke machine out for Pepsi. All that really mattered was that, once again, she was on the outside looking in. Literally. She wasn't at the kids' table; she wasn't even at the party.

The office's resident fiddle player, Brian, was standing at the whiteboard, gesticulating at something he'd written. Lussi couldn't read what was on the board—her contacts helped her vision, but they didn't give her superpowers. He paused and looked straight at her. The rest of the room followed suit. Lussi raised her hand to give them a little wave. No one waved back. Instead, Sloppy Joe came to the window and, with a dead-eyed glare, snapped the blinds shut.

CHAPTER SEVENTEEN

Lussi marched back to her office with the Percht. To anyone who might have caught sight of her, she probably looked like an angry kid stomping back to her room with her stuffed animal. Which wouldn't have been far from the truth. She put an extra *oomph* into her step as she mounted the winding staircase, pounding the steps like an asshole neighbor. Halfway down the third-floor hallway, however, she stopped.

The door to the art department was open.

It was the first time she'd had a chance to see inside Stanley's office, and now she knew why: the place was a disaster area. Charcoal drawings covered the peeling wallpaper; the paisley print was completely blacked out in spots. Art supplies were stacked on every available surface—easels, a light box, several desks. One chair was buried beneath a tower of galleys. It didn't seem possible to work in such conditions. Then again, it was to be expected. You couldn't cage an artist inside a publishing house and expect them to suddenly behave by society's rules.

A rough watercolor of the Richard Yates cover was sitting on an easel. Stanley was in the meeting downstairs. It couldn't hurt to take a quick peek . . .

She slipped into the room for a closer look. The human skull was a huge improvement. They were really going to go with her suggestion. She couldn't wait to see the final version—Stanley had farmed it out to a freelance artist, and they expected the piece to come in later this week. The Raven had torn into him at a follow-up meeting with a long diatribe about the importance of adhering to the schedule. Although normally sullen and withdrawn, his face had grown redder and redder until it looked like he needed to be juiced like Violet Beauregarde in *Willy Wonka*.

"What are you doing in here?"

Lussi whipped around. Stanley was in the doorway, a despondent look on his face.

"Sorry, the door was open and I wanted to take a look at the cover design. I think it's brilliant. The colors . . ."

He wasn't listening to her. He hurried to his desk, where he plucked a pencil out of a coffee mug full of writing utensils. He examined it closely then tossed it over his shoulder. All Lussi could do was watch as he emptied the mug. Still not finding what he was after, he opened the top drawer of the desk. Lussi was afraid he was after a firearm—the receptionist couldn't be the only one around this office locked and loaded—but after a fruitless search, he slammed it shut. He pointed a trembling finger in her direction. Lussi inched backward. She was about to run when he dropped to his knees and buried his face in his hands.

"Norma," he wailed. "What did you do with her?"

Lussi wasn't sure how to respond. Here was a man old enough to be her grandfather, bawling like a toddler who'd lost his blankie. He'd seen action in the Korean War, according to Sloppy Joe. Everyone in the office carried around shadows of former lives, which she only glimpsed here and there. Was he having some sort of flashback?

She knelt beside the art director. She reached for him, but then thought better of it. Instead, she lightly patted the air a safe distance from his back. "Tell me about Norma."

"You tried to take her the other day," he said between muffled sobs. "You just couldn't keep your hands off her, could you?" A large snot bubble had formed in one nostril and was about to pop. "We've been together since I was at Random House. Doesn't that mean anything to you?"

The Raven was at the door now. She was sipping a hot cup of joe with a look of amusement. The Raven caught Lussi's eye and nodded to the hallway. They closed the door on Stanley, who had curled into a fetal position.

"Done with the meeting?" Lussi asked her, doing little to disguise her sarcasm.

The Raven ignored her remark. "What did you do to him?"

"What did *I* do? The door was open. All I wanted was a closer look at the Yates mock-up. Then he storms in, and flies off the handle about some girl named 'Norma,' accusing me of trying to steal her away from him."

The Raven held up a chrome mechanical pencil, the same one Lussi had found on the floor last Monday. "Meet Norma. He left her in the conference room."

Lussi closed her eyes and tried to find her Zen. She knew men named their penises, but this was ridiculous.

"You're not about to cry, too, are you?" The Raven asked, her tone just this side of patronizing. "We don't need two sobbing messes around here."

Lussi forced a smile. "I don't cry at work. I save it for when I get home, like a regular goddamn person."

The Raven snort-laughed. She put a hand on Lussi's shoulder. "Here's what we do. If you try to apologize now—"

"For what?"

"How would you like it if someone trespassed in your office?"

"They do all the time!" Several more office doors were cracked open now. They had an audience. She lowered her voice. "Fine. I'll apologize. And then I'm going to stick that damn thing where the sun doesn't shine."

The Raven tried to shoot her a disapproving look but couldn't keep a straight face. She rolled the pencil under Stanley's door. "Give him a few hours," The Raven said, rising to her feet. "This isn't the first time this has happened. Won't be the last. But if you want to be part of this company, you'll need to learn to work with people. And some of them are . . . difficult."

They walked together down the hall to where the editorial offices were located. "Wait a minute," Lussi said, halting. "Where's Cal?"

The Raven looked at her, puzzled.

"The intern? The young man you borrowed?"

"Oh, Calumet. I just sent him to Midtown to fetch a manuscript."

"His leg is broken."

"He has crutches," The Raven said. "And excellent upper body strength."

"They couldn't overnight you the manuscript? If he gets hurt again . . ."

"He'll be fine. And, as I'm sure you've noticed, the mail in this neighborhood can be . . . unreliable. Erratic." The Raven smirked. "Although, between you, me, and the partridge in the pear tree, the mailman also sells *primo* Mary Jane."

———

Lussi slumped in her chair, her energy sapped. She found the plastic vampire teeth in her drawer and fit them into her mouth. They were sized for a child; the uneven plastic on the edges dug into her gums. It was the closest thing to a stress ball she had.

Today was turning out to be another one of those days. She swiveled in her desk chair to look at her bookshelves behind her desk and saw the empty spot where she'd placed the Percht after the holiday party. Damn it. She'd set it down on the light box in the art department. She'd have to figure out a way to snatch it back later. But there was something else she was forgetting. The coffee. She'd been brewing a fresh pot before she went out on the fire escape and got sidetracked by that stupid secret meeting.

She raced down to the break room, taking the stairs by twos.

Not that it mattered. When she got there, the pot was empty.

The meeting had cleared out, and everyone had descended on the coffee machine like fire ants on a sleeping baby. And, of course, no one had started another pot.

She dug her nails into her palms. Her patience had worn as thin as the veil between worlds on All Hallows' Eve. Mercurial artists. Clandestine meetings. Trigger-happy receptionists. Small mammals in serious need of house training. Lunch thieves. Pranksters. The more she ran over the past week in her mind, the more she felt herself slipping into darkness.

All she wanted was a simple cup of coffee. Black, no sugar.

Brian rounded the corner, whistling some long-forgotten battle hymn. He had a Styrofoam McDonald's coffee cup in one hand. He walked right past Lussi to the Coffee-mate jar and set his cup on the counter. As he was unscrewing the creamer's lid, he glanced over at Lussi. When he saw how intensely she was staring at the empty pot, he slowly set the creamer back down.

"Someone drink the last of the coffee?" he asked. "I hate that, don't you?"

She hissed at him, baring the plastic teeth.

He pushed the McDonald's cup toward her and backed up as if she were as unhinged as Stanley. "Here. I haven't touched it," he stammered. "I . . . probably shouldn't have caffeine past noon anyway."

She tried to explain she was only playing around, but her words were garbled. By the time she spat the fangs out, Brian had already ducked out. Was he really afraid of her? She was pint-sized. She'd never been in a fight in her life. He must have felt the anger radiating off her like steam from a sewer grate. She wasn't herself lately.

Lussi took Brian's coffee back to her office, because, hey, coffee was coffee. She wondered whether it wasn't simply time to cut and run. She needed a job, but not this bad. She could always return to waitressing. She settled into her desk and stared at the stack of manuscripts that she'd already read . . . and then at the larger stack in the corner of her office. Reading submissions while angry was rarely a good idea. Then she remembered she still had Fabien's book in her handbag. She turned to the first page.

CHAPTER EIGHTEEN

By the time she looked up from Fabien's manuscript, it was five thirty. She took a break to hit the restroom. His book was good—better than good. It was *great. Transylvanian Dirt* was, as he'd told her, the best thing he'd ever written. A page-turner that transported her far away from all the office drama for a few hours. She was only a hundred sixty pages in, but already she could smell a best seller. Even the clichéd World War II prologue worked. Had the book she'd been looking for been right under her nose? She'd have to finish it first, but she felt something she hadn't felt in a long time: hope.

On the way back to her office, she peered over the railing into the lobby. Gail had already gone home for the day. Down the hall, the light was still on under the art department door. She would wait for Stanley to head home, then slip into his office to take back the Percht. If the door was unlocked, that was. She had no experience picking locks.

When she got within earshot of her own office, she heard the phone ringing. She rushed to answer it. "Lussi Meyer, Broken—sorry, *Blackwood*-Patterson," she said.

"Want me to hang up and call again so you can do that over?"

Lussi sighed. It wasn't an agent with a hot manuscript. It was only her sister, returning her call from last week. "Why don't you hang up and I'll call you back—free long distance," Lussi said. "Perks of having an office job again."

"I'm talking to you on Friends and Family, don't worry," her sister said. "It wouldn't hurt you to get a home phone, but anyway, congrats on the job. It sounds like a great company to work for—we have scads of Blackwood books in the high school library."

But does anyone check them out? Lussi wanted to ask. She stretched the phone cord to the window.

Kiera taught sixth-grade home economics, and filled Lussi in on some drama with the teacher's union and gossip from their hometown. Lussi only half followed what she was saying. She was busy looking out the window to see if Stanley had left the building yet. As the last of the sunlight faded, the trash cans in the park burned brighter. Among the brambles, deeper into the park, she saw the silhouette of a man in a fedora. Peter Faber. Was he watching her? She could no longer tell friend from foe. Before moving to the city, she'd been warned that the parks were no place for a young woman. No matter how inviting they looked during the day, they transformed at night like werewolves under a full moon.

The same could be said for some buildings.

". . . I should get going," her sister was saying. "Syd's been quiet too long. She's probably gotten into something. She's at that age . . ."

Lussi was about to ask about her niece, but the sight of the empty gift box next to the wastebasket reminded her there was another reason she needed to talk to her sister. "Before you go, I have kind of a weird question. Do you remember Perky?"

There was a pause. Lussi thought she'd lost her, but her sister finally answered. "Don't even think about getting one of those things for Syd. Unless you're willing to sit up with her at night when she wakes screaming. She's not like we were at that age. Kids these days are a lot different. They're not as tough."

"It's not another Cabbage Patch situation, if that's what you're worried about." Last year, Lussi had bought her niece a bootleg Cabbage Patch Kid in Chinatown. Thankfully, the rash on her niece's chest was short-lived.

"Leave the toys to Santa," Kiera said. "He's a professional."

"I was just wondering if you know what happened to Oma's doll. I know we sold a lot of stuff in the garage sale, after the—after the funeral."

"You don't remember."

"I was, like, four," Lussi said. "All I've got are bits and pieces. Tiny memories. The funeral is a blur. All I remember is the make-up on her face. She looked like a clown."

"You were five when she passed away, but you're lucky if that's all you remember. I was old enough—I knew Santa wasn't real, and all that. You, on the other hand, had trouble differentiating fact from fiction. Mom was afraid Oma was going to scar you for life with her folk stories. That was basically the reason Mom wouldn't let her speak German in our house."

"There are worse things than scars."

"If you say so. Syd's the same way you were—she'll believe anything we tell her. We have to be careful."

"A girl after my own heart," Lussi said.

Kiera laughed. "Let's hope not. One writer in the family is enough."

Lussi let the comment slide, as she always did. "Why did she bring the doll with her? To America, I mean. Of all the things she could have brought with her, why that?"

Her sister sighed into the phone. "It was the middle of a war. Her husband had died. She was pregnant with Dad. Maybe she just wanted something to remind her of home." Another silence. Then: "I don't know what happened to it, but if it's still around it's in Mom and Dad's basement. Who, by the way, keep asking if you're coming home this year."

"I'll call them when I know for sure," Lussi said. After they said their goodbyes, Lussi noted the time. It was past six. Dusk was fading into night. Lussi hadn't seen Stanley exit the building yet. Not unless he'd taken the fire escape, leaving through the alley like Tom Cruise trying to avoid a throng of fans on the sidewalk.

But when she checked in the hall, there was no light coming from under the door to the art department. She stopped and reached for the knob. It turned when she tested it. Unlocked. Perfect. She looked both ways down the hall. Empty. The building had all but cleared out; night had moved in. She was about to give the knob a quick twist when a muffled cough from inside sent her leaping back.

Stanley was waiting for her in the dark.

Had he known she was going to come back for the Percht? It didn't seem possible. He couldn't have known for sure the doll was even hers—nobody had so much as glimpsed it inside that box. More likely, he was lying in wait for her to make another pass at his girl.

This man was patently deranged.

Lussi crammed the rest of Fabien's book into her handbag. She'd talk to Digby about the Stanley situation tomorrow. See if the three of them could sit down and talk through all of this like adults. Maybe he'd even confess to hazing her. Wouldn't that be nice? Two birds, one stone. She made sure to lock the door to her office, jiggling the knob. When she reached the stairs, she turned back and rechecked her office door. Still locked. She didn't want to come in tomorrow to find another person waiting for her—or another surprise on her floor.

CHAPTER NINETEEN

When Lussi returned to work the next morning, the entire staff of Blackwood-Patterson was assembled in the lobby. Xavier Blackwood's funeral was that morning. She'd forgotten all about it, with all the excitement from yesterday. Lussi had never been so glad to be a conservative dresser—thank God she wasn't wearing a yellow jumper or something. Her coworkers were milling around, chatting quietly, respectfully, as if not to wake the man napping in the casket uptown. She didn't see Stanley. It occurred to her that he might have called in sick today, on account of what happened yesterday. If so, she hoped a day of rest would help him pull himself together.

Lussi approached Rachael, who was watching the snow fall through one of the picture windows. The iron bars cast long shadows on the woman's face. "Have you seen Stanley this morning?" Lussi asked. Since Rachael was the designer, she was the one who worked closest with the art director.

Rachael shrugged. "Haven't seen him. Bet he's driving separately. He lives out on Long Island. Hates public transportation. Says he'd rather die in a car crash than set foot in a subway car."

"Seems rather extreme."

"Can you blame him, though?" Rachael said, turning to her. "Whenever I take the train, the smell follows me around the rest of the day. Perspiration and motor oil, with undertones of warm urine."

That was how the whole of Manhattan smelled, Lussi thought. There wasn't any way to avoid it getting in your hair. She felt a tap at her shoulder. The Raven. "Could I have a word with you, Lussi?"

People were beginning to file out the door. A rented bus was sitting outside, idling now. Lussi was in her winter boots. She had to run up to her office to change and then return before the bus left. "Can it wait?" she asked.

"Actually, no," The Raven said. "I have a box of galleys arriving from FedEx today at around ten. I need somebody to stay back to sign for the package. You can't just leave a package on the steps in this neighborhood, not with those . . . well, those people out there. Besides, you didn't *know* Mr. Blackwood. You'd be doing me a huge favor."

Lussi was speechless. Half the staff was already out the door, including Gail, whose *job* it was to sign for packages. She watched Cal hobble his way toward the door, the rubber stoppers on his crutches squeaking on the tile. The venue would be packed with hundreds of publishing celebrities—authors, editors, agents. Everyone from Andrew Wylie to Sterling Lord. A few of her old colleagues. Definitely some agents who'd been avoiding her calls. If she stayed here until midmorning, she would miss the entire service. And possibly the reception. The Raven sounded sincere, though. Perhaps there was a way for Lussi to turn this to her advantage.

"So I've got this smoking-hot manuscript I'd like to get your take on," Lussi said. "Like, Chernobyl hot. If you promise to look at it when you return, I'll wait here until your package arrives. What do you say?"

The Raven put a hand on Lussi's shoulder and gave it a squeeze. "You're such a doll."

Lussi held the door as the last of her colleagues filed out, then locked every one of its thirteen locks by hand. She took off her boots and climbed the stairs, barefoot, to change into her flats. If The Raven refused to pass Fabien's book along to Digby, that would be it. She would walk out the door. Never look back. Leave the Blackwood Building in the past, where it belonged. *Transylvanian Dirt* was a triumph. Lussi needed to start acquisitions talks now, before his agent started shopping it around town.

———

Lussi's office door was locked. Just as she'd left it. She went to the break room to check the coffee situation. Not only was the coffeemaker unplugged but the Folgers can was empty. There was a Russian deli on the corner. All she needed was a little jump start to her day. She threw her jacket on and headed outside. She'd be gone all of five minutes.

An inch of snow had fallen this morning; today it was sticking. Tompkins Square Park looked more like a real park now that it had snow cover. The number of people who called the park home hadn't diminished. According to Sloppy Joe, the city routinely cleared the tents. Health and safety regulations. Within hours, a new encampment sprung up from the ashes. It wasn't solely the homeless who bothered the mayor, though. The park was also ground zero for protests. Lussi could read some of the signs when the protestors lined the sidewalk, shouting at passing cars. FIGHT AIDS NOT GAYS. JUST SAY NO TO TRUMP CITY. When the police cracked down, they didn't differentiate between protestors and the homeless, between the gutter punks in their studded denim jackets and the beatniks reading poetry through megaphones. They wanted blood any way they could get it.

So, too, did the weather today. It was twenty degrees, even colder with the windchill. It was supposed to fall into the single digits overnight, according to *Good Morning America*. Not that Lussi entirely trusted meteorologists. She regarded their methods as iffy. They were only slightly more reliable than astrologists.

She paid for her coffee and headed back. A panhandler started following her, shouting something unintelligible. He had wandered across Avenue A to Blackwood-Patterson's side of the street. If she had anything to give the crusty-looking man with frost in his eyebrows, she would have. She owed her roommate for the past two months' rent, and her first paycheck wouldn't be cut until Friday. Her wallet was running on fumes until then. This would be her last coffee of the week. It was a lot to explain, so she just mumbled an apology and kept moving.

The man eventually stopped tailing her.

The Blackwood Building's steps were bare except for salt to melt the ice. No note on the door. FedEx hadn't come yet. She punched in her code on the keypad and slipped into the black brownstone, which seemed to swallow her up.

The door to the art department was shut. Natural light filtered underneath it into the hall from the window inside. Now was her chance to get in and out without any fear of walking in on Stanley. She set her coffee on the carpet. She pressed her ear to the door, listened. She didn't know who or what she was listening for because Stanley wasn't here. It never hurt to be cautious, though.

When she was satisfied that the quietude was for real, she tried the knob.

The door opened easily.

Stanley was seated on a tall black stool at the easel with the Yates cover. His back was toward her. The door continued to swing inward, and she reached for the knob to pull it closed but it was too late.

There was a dull thud as the door hit something solid, a book-shelf or a desk that had been placed too close behind it. Lussi stood there, exposed, waiting for Stanley to turn around and chase her out.

Except something curious happened: he didn't swing around. In fact, he didn't acknowledge her at all. His left hand was down by his side, twitching.

"Stanley?"

No answer. She tiptoed toward him. She didn't think he was baiting her. Something was seriously wrong here.

She touched his shoulder. He didn't seem to register her touch, but it set him spinning around in the chair, inch by inch, until he was facing her. His pupils were large as basketballs. He was staring at her like an infant. Curious, uncomprehending. Both his chin and white button-down were dotted with a reddish-brown spray. Dried blood. He'd had a nosebleed—a bad one. Wouldn't be the first art director to get coked out of his gourd at the office.

She looked around the office for some tissues and saw the Percht where she'd left it. Right there, untouched, on his desk. Perky could only grin at her with its carved, dagger-like teeth.

"Let's get you cleaned up, Stanley."

Stanley coughed hard, misting her face with blood. She recoiled and quickly wiped it out of her eyes with her shirt. He issued a guttural moan, like a wailing ghost. She got the impression he wasn't actually seeing her—he was far away, maybe in some Asian jungle. Must have scored some really bad shit.

The sunlight caught something in his left nostril. A glint of chrome, poking out of his nose, barely visible through the dried blood.

Her stomach dropped out like a soldier kicked out of a plane without a chute.

There wasn't something sticking out of his nose.

There was something sticking *into* his nose.

Norma.

CHAPTER TWENTY

Zelda Fitzgerald had once phoned the fire department to report a fire. When the firefighters arrived at her hotel room, she greeted them at the door. They couldn't see or smell any smoke. *Where's the fire?* they asked.

Here, Zelda said, tapping her chest emphatically. *Right here.*

Zelda Fitzgerald was, in fact, clinically insane, but her confidence was inspiring. Lussi wished she could have summoned some of the woman's chutzpah to help her deal with the Stanley situation. She'd felt faintly embarrassed to dial 9-1-1, struggling to describe "the nature of her emergency" (as the operator kept repeating). She'd led the police officers upstairs to the art department, at which point her ability to form words—let alone sentences—left her completely. Unable to articulate herself, she'd simply pointed at the zombie on the swivel chair. He was alive and not alive. It wasn't until she stepped outside for some fresh air that she realized she'd been crying the entire time. The tears on her cheeks turned to ice slicks. They melted at her touch.

Lussi waited outside on the sidewalk in the cold. Emergency personnel were weaving in and out of the building through the propped door. None of her coworkers had returned. She'd left a message on an answering machine at the Carnegie box office but doubted anyone would get it. Lussi's teeth were chattering like an express train on a straightaway. There was no way she was going back inside that building, though. Not after what she'd seen.

"You look like you've seen a ghost," she heard a friendly voice say from behind her.

She turned. It was Fabien with a messenger bag slung over his shoulder. He was dressed in so many layers that his arms floated beside him at forty-five-degree angles. She couldn't smell his cologne, at least; her nostrils were frozen shut.

"I wish I'd seen a ghost," Lussi said. "I could probably handle that."

They watched as the paramedics hauled Stanley down the stairs on a gurney, his long legs bent, his shirt unbuttoned. His face pale as a sheet of typing paper. The tip of the mechanical pencil was still poking out of his nostril.

Lussi filled Fabien in on what had happened, even though what had happened was still a little foggy to her. All signs pointed to Stanley shoving the pencil up his own nose. Nobody had accused Lussi of being involved, but she couldn't shake the feeling that it had something to do with her. "I said I was going to 'stick it where the sun doesn't shine,' or something like that. I didn't *mean* it."

"Don't beat yourself up about it. I keep asking God to smite my enemies. Does He listen?" He shook his head.

"You don't believe in God."

"Not until I see some smiting." Fabien patted his bag. "I came by to see if I could pick my book up—need to get it to my agent this afternoon. Although this appears to be a bad time."

A fire truck rolled to a gentle stop, parking alongside the ambulance and trio of police cruisers. Two firemen, bulked up in their yellow-and-gray jackets, hopped off. The looks on their faces told her they knew they were late to the party. With the situation under control, they'd gotten dressed up for nothing. She knew the feeling.

Lussi turned back to Fabien. "I don't know how much longer I can take all of . . . this. Not just what's happened today, but what's been happening."

"What else did I miss?"

She filled him in on Cal's injury, and the hazing. For the first time, she wondered if whoever was targeting her hadn't also targeted Cal. What if his accident wasn't an accident? He had no memory of what preceded the incident, due to his concussion. "And I forgot to tell you the night of the party, but we have a mystery shitter."

He raised his eyebrows.

"It's exactly what it sounds like," she said. "Supposedly, it's a raccoon. But honestly, who knows? When you're dealing with somebody devious enough to steal a fruitcake, all bets are off. At least I can safely cross Stanley off the list of possible pranksters."

"You have a list."

"It's not written down." She tapped her temple. "It's all up here."

Fabien rubbed his mittens together and blew into them. "This whole conspiracy might all be up there. You're the sanest person I know, but this city was bound to grind you down at some point. You're also, what, in your mid-twenties? Statistically speaking, that's when schizophrenics develop their first symptoms."

Fabien Nightingale wasn't somebody you went to for a pep talk. If you told him you felt fat, he'd tell you that you looked fat, too.

"I don't think I'm imagining things," she said. "I think this is all connected to my Secret Santa. You saw Perky. You saw the doll my Secret Santa gave me. Somebody was trying to send me a message."

"Perhaps," Fabien said. "They may also have given it to you for protection. Didn't you say these Perchten have special properties? Maybe you should write that list down. Could help you narrow down the suspects."

It was an idea. She could find some way to ask Gail who else might have been in the Blackwood-Patterson offices over the past two weeks. The OSHA inspector had said she was in danger. Could he have somehow gained access to the building and dropped the gift off for her?

"I'll think about it," she said, without the same conviction she might have had yesterday. Now that the seriousness of what had happened to Stanley was setting in, her own problems suddenly didn't seem all that terrible. Not when compared to a self-administered lobotomy. "About your book . . ."

She wanted to tell him to have his agent hold off on sending it out wide, that she wanted to make an offer . . . except she couldn't say that. She was in no position to make promises. There were the internal politics she'd have to maneuver, not to mention the company's finances. Blackwood-Patterson was on the cusp of ruin. Had been for its entire existence. Even if she could make a sizeable offer on *Transylvanian Dirt*, there was a chance the financing Digby was seeking would fall through. Digby had seemed so confident in their early discussions, she hadn't questioned his ability to deliver. After the other night—seeing him blitzed in the basement, hallucinating his dead father—doubt had begun to creep into her mind.

She was staring off into the distance at nothing in particular when she saw him. A trench-coat-clad figure in a fedora on the opposite sidewalk. Peter Faber.

"I've got to go," she told Fabien, breaking away into the street. Lussi snaked through the parked emergency vehicles and idling cars, following Peter. Traffic was being rerouted, but it was slow going. Horns honking, sirens blaring. Shouts in every direction,

Fabien's voice among them.

Lussi weaved her way through the chaos. Fabien's shouts grew farther and farther away. At the park's entrance, Peter disappeared down a snow-covered pathway. She followed and the park denizens parted like the sea for Moses. She couldn't run very fast on account of the snow, but she didn't have to. He was deliberately walking slowly enough for her to keep pace. They were in a slow-motion chase. Lussi rounded a thatch of fallen trees and saw where he was headed. He was leading her to the deepest recesses of the park, where the fires burned brightest.

CHAPTER TWENTY-ONE

Lussi entered a communal area where the junkies, home-
less, and gutter punks mixed in the center of Tompkins Square
Park. She moved among them, a ghost in their tent city. They ignored her except for brief glances. She scanned the park for the
man who called himself Peter Faber, but had lost sight of him.
Fires roared in the rusted trash cans, the same fires she'd watched
burn from her office window. They had never looked this inviting
before, but now she'd passed the point of being cold—a bad sign.
Her thin jacket was no match for the falling temperature.

A group of men made space for her at a barrel. Just walking past
any one of these men in their muddied clothes on the street would
have had her picking up her pace, but here she was. She warmed
her hands at the flames. Somebody wrapped a blanket around her
like a cloak. Did any of them recognize her from the third-floor
window across the street? Did they sense she was an outcast herself, albeit of a different variety? They were all broken toys here,
like on that island in the *Rudolph* special, the one Fabien had once
tried to convince her was an allegory for homosexuality. (It was
hardly an allegory, she'd argued—the dentist elf was as queer as
Boy George.) Many of the park's permanent residents sipped from

airplane bottles of liquor; several openly sucked foul-smelling smoke from what she could only assume were crack pipes.

"So," Peter said, joining her at the barrel. "Believe me now?"

—

Lussi felt for the man's business card in her pocket. The two of them were alone at the fire. They'd been given space. Lussi didn't know what sort of power this man wielded around here. He walked in more than one world, though. Her fingers had just enough feeling that she could grasp the card. "Fred Munson," she read. "Religion editor, Random House." She paused. "This is you?"

"I have some fake OSHA cards but I handed you one of my real ones. Thought for sure you'd figured me out and would've called by now."

"I've kind of been busy. But I'm sure you know all about that."

He shook his head. "I have a full-time job uptown. I don't have all day to watch over you and make sure you're safe."

"I never asked you to."

"You didn't trail me into the park to tell me to fuck off."

"Fuck off," she said.

He laughed. "Fair enough. I deserve that. I should have been up-front with you, but I didn't know if I could trust you. Full disclosure, I used to be an associate editor at Blackwood-Patterson. I doubt anyone remembers me—"

"You're Frederick."

He glanced at her. The flames danced in his wide eyes. "They still talk about me, huh?"

"You could say that." Lussi wasn't sure how much she wanted to reveal. She needed to hear more. He hadn't earned her trust yet. He'd earned this meeting, but that was it. "You're not a ghost, are you? Because if you are, you have to tell me. It's a rule."

"Do I look like a ghost?"

"I've never seen one."

"I'm not a ghost, no. Were you expecting a spectral visitation today?"

"Just curious," she said. "A lot of weird shit has been happening lately. Tell me, though, why you would want to help me? You don't even know me. I could be a terrible person. The type of person who steals a coworker's lunch out of the fridge."

He lowered his head, closed his eyes. "I'm just somebody who used to be where you are—confused, scared. Trying to make sense of things." He fixed his gaze on her. "You're in a stronger position than I ever was. Maybe you can even do something about it. You're asking the right questions, at least."

It was close to noon. She would have to return shortly. She owed Fabien an explanation. And she owed her coworkers an explanation, too, before somebody stumbled upon the blood-spattered art department.

"Let's hear it, then," she told him. "The Cliff's Notes version, preferably."

━━

Frederick—aka Fred, aka Peter—had attended a Jesuit seminary, but the priesthood wasn't for him. "A professor suggested I try publishing, thought I had an eye for parsing the texts," he said. "Turns out he'd been in the army with Xavier Blackwood. He slipped him my resume. The timing couldn't have been better—they were starting a religion imprint under their nonfiction banner, Swan Creek."

"How long ago was this?"

"Not long. I've been told I have a baby face." He grinned. Not even a smile line around his eyes.

By the end of his first week at Blackwood, he said, he sensed a strangeness. The other employees were detached, distant. When he smiled at them, they looked away. "I thought maybe they didn't like brothers," he said with a laugh, although it was clear to Lussi he wasn't kidding. "Publishing is a pretty white industry. Of course, I'm not telling you anything you don't already know."

Lussi thought of the one Black guy in sales at Broken Angel. That was considered a *diverse* workplace.

"Took a while for the other employees to embrace me. After that initial bumpy patch, I started to feel more like a part of the company. Can't say I ever fit in, but as you've no doubt guessed, Blackwood–Patterson takes square pegs and fits them into round holes."

"This bumpy patch at the beginning. Were you, how do I put this . . . were you hazed?"

Frederick was silent for a moment. The honking and the sirens and the shouting continued in the distance. Finally, he fixed his gaze on her. "Alan."

The maintenance man had the run of the building. He had a key to every office. Of course—

"You know who I'm talking about then," Frederick said, reading her expression. "I'm hesitant to say anything, because I don't like telling tales out of school. That man has a wicked streak . . . but I don't think he's the root cause of what's happening in that building."

Her sense of relief withered and died.

Frederick looked to the sky, which had grown overcast. The deluge of precipitation had slowed to a trickle. Lussi wondered if anyone had returned from the funeral reception yet, and if they could pick her out of the crowded area.

"Do you know the story behind the bars on the building?" he asked.

She shook her head. "Just that they might repel evil spirits. If you believe in that sort of thing."

"The East Village used to be known as Little Germany," Frederick said, gesturing around them. "Almost every old building in this neighborhood was either built, owned, or rented at the time by first- and second-generation German Americans. Like all immigrants, they brought their own folklore . . . including curious beliefs about iron and silver. Those two metals were said to be uniquely suited to repelling ghosts and other malevolent entities."

Industrialist Theobold Ottomar Wagner constructed the edifice now known as the Blackwood Building in the late 1800s, he explained. Wagner, being a superstitious man like every other rich prick, paid top dollar to protect himself and his fortune from enemies both real and imagined—including ones of the supernatural persuasion. "The rich live in constant fear of being destitute," Frederick said. "As they should."

"You're saying that spirits can't break into the building," Lussi said. "Because of the iron."

"I'm saying Theobold Ottomar Wagner believed that." He fixed his gaze on her. "And if there's any truth to the folklore, it also stands to reason that the bars could trap evil within the building. I worked there for two and a half months—didn't even make it to ninety days. The evil that I felt . . ." He shook his head. "I started digging into the building's past, looking into strange accidents and disappearances. Asking questions. The wrong questions, apparently. They let me go."

"You believe evil has a physical presence that can be trapped."

"The Church's *Catechism* says that evil is the absence of good, and that—"

"Not the Church," she said. "I asked what you believe."

Frederick reached into the inner pockets of his trench coat. Lussi tensed until she saw him produce a book wrapped in kraft paper. He passed it to her. "Do not bring detestable things into your home, for then you will be destroyed, just like them."

He tipped his cap to her and was gone before she could stop him.

CHAPTER TWENTY-TWO

The emergency vehicles had departed by the time Lussi re-
turned to the Blackwood Building. The door was closed and Gail
wasn't at the front desk. "Anyone here?" Lussi yelled in the lobby,
her voice bouncing back from the upper reaches of the atrium. No
response other than the echo of her own voice. The reception must
have still been going on. No telling how long the literati would
hold court if there was an open bar.

She sat in Gail's chair. From the front desk, she could keep an
eye on the door. Better to check out Frederick's book here, than
to get lost reading it in her office and have someone surprise her.

She fished the wrapped book out of her jacket. It would have
been nice if Frederick had given her some hint about the book,
but he hadn't. She'd come across a fair number of occult texts in
her day. They were a staple of horror fiction. Real-life occult books
always disappointed, though. They were less repositories of forbid-
den knowledge and more repositories of bad writing.

Lussi unwrapped the book. It was a cracked black leather hard-
back. According to the gold lettering on the cover, it was . . . a
Bible? This was the "detestable thing" he'd warned her not to take
home? She hadn't expected the Egyptian *Book of the Dead*, but this

was the literary equivalent of receiving a sweater for Christmas.

The title page indicated it was printed in 1924. The interior pages were in remarkably decent condition for a book over sixty years old—no yellowing, though the gilt edges had been mostly rubbed off. Still, it was impressive. Lussi had mass-market paperbacks from the late seventies that had already fallen to pieces.

There was a clatter above her head inside the ceiling. It almost sounded like somebody was kicking boxes around in the attic.

"You're not a ghost," she said loud enough so the not-ghost could hear her. "You're just a raccoon. So shut up—I'm trying to read down here."

The noise stopped.

She fanned the pages. Nothing out of the ordinary about it. She hadn't been wrong about him—he had wanted to protect her, but not with a pagan doll. With a Bible. If he'd only told her what it was, she could have saved him the trouble—Lussi had a Bible at home. It was gathering dust, but she had one. She really, really didn't need a second copy.

The sound of the locks disengaging woke her, as if from a deep sleep. "Shit, shit, shit," she said, stuffing the Bible into her jacket. She sat up straight, crossing her hands on the desk. No, in her lap. No, on the desk. She did her best to wipe the guilty look off her face as The Raven entered.

The editor in chief spied Lussi and went straight for her. She was clutching a book in her hand, waving it in front of her face as if to dispel some unseen evil. "What happened in here? It smells like a campfire."

"Does it?" Lussi said. She sniffed her shirt. It smelled faintly of smoke.

The Raven slapped the book down on the desk with a *thwap*. "And what is this?"

Lussi picked it up, a trade paperback that felt cheap in her hands. *A Cannibal in Manhattan* by Tama Janowitz. In small type in the corner, it said, ADVANCE READING COPY. NOT FOR SALE. Lussi slapped her forehead. "This isn't . . ."

"The galleys you were supposed to be watching for?" The Raven said, removing her gloves. "I found that on a vagrant's blanket down the street, on top of a pile of used books. It was the only copy, so Lord knows what happened to the rest. I had to pay him seventy-five cents out of my own pocket. Wait . . . is that blood in your hair, Lussi?"

◢━━

After The Raven heard what had happened to Stanley, she insisted Lussi take the rest of the afternoon off. "I'll make sure we get a cleaning crew in here to take care of the art department," The Raven said. She ran a finger over the desk, leaving a clear trail through the buildup of dust and dirt. "Maybe they can tidy up the rest of this place, too." She told Lussi not to worry about the galleys. They were replaceable. Lussi's suddenly fragile sanity was not.

Lussi did not mention Frederick.

CHAPTER TWENTY-THREE

When Lussi entered her apartment, she tripped over a stack of books inside the entryway, sending them flying. She picked herself up off the carpet—the deep shag had cushioned her fall. She'd been meaning to take the books to the office to fill out her bookshelves. Anything to free up space in her apartment without actually getting rid of any books. In her next apartment—preferably not on Satan Island—she would invest in proper bookshelves. No more hand-me-down plywood shelves from the curb. Trouble was, no amount of shelving would ever be enough. She worked in publishing—when she returned home and brushed her hair, books tumbled out.

Lussi shrugged off her coat. She laid on the living room couch and was immediately pounced on by her tabby.

"Not tonight, Radcliffe," Lussi said, giving him a tiny scratch behind the ears. She set all twelve pounds of him down onto the carpet as gently as she could. Radcliffe stood on his tiptoes, peering over the couch at her, examining her. Did he smell the blood in her hair? The cat remembered he had somewhere important to be and shot off down the hall.

"That's right," Lussi said. "Go paw at Casey's door." Her roommate had taken the train to Philly on Sunday to see her boyfriend. She wouldn't be home until later in the week.

From the couch, Lussi had an unobstructed view of the city—the Empire State Building, the Chrysler Building, the Twin Towers. She couldn't see the Blackwood Building from here but it loomed over the entire city in her mind, casting a long, sinister shadow.

The dark side of life had always fascinated her. It may have started with Oma's stories, but the first real imprints on her brain were in stark black-and-white: Dracula. The Mummy. Franken-stein's monster. Some of her fondest memories from childhood were of watching those old Universal creature features with her dad on Saturday nights. It was a thrill she'd also found in the short stories of Poe and Lovecraft. At no point, however, had she ever believed any of the supernatural stuff was real. She never worried there was a monster under the bed—though, if there had been, it would have *ruled*.

At least that's what she thought at the time.

Now she wasn't so sure. When faced with strangers warning her that her life was in danger and coworkers bleeding all over her, she wasn't sure at all.

——

After showering, Lussi dialed Fabien on her roommate's hot dog phone. She didn't like to go into Casey's bedroom when she wasn't home, but these were extenuating circumstances.

"Hello?" Fabien answered. He sounded groggy, like he'd just woken up.

She told him she needed to talk to him. In person. She wanted to show him the Bible, which she'd left at the office out of an abundance of caution. See if Fabien noticed anything unusual about it. He was something of an expert on unusual books. The last thing she wanted to do was involve any of her friends now working at other publishing houses. They would think she was—

"Crazy? You mean like someone who dashes into traffic during an otherwise ordinary conversation, disappears into a wooded expanse, and doesn't return?"

She apologized profusely, but he told her not to worry. "Here's the situation, though: I've already left the house once today. I'm not keen to do it again. There are too many tourists out and about—it's like they've never seen snow before. *Hey, honey, let's take a holiday with the kids to the city! We'll see that big ol' Christmas tree, take in a Broadway matinee, and let our children sit on a stranger's lap at Macy's.*"

She switched the phone from one ear to the other. Talking into a plastic hot dog bun was not very comfortable. "How about the library on Fifth and Forty-second? The one with the lions out front."

"Patience and Fortitude," he said. "That's the research branch, you know. And this is the week before finals. It will be crawling with college students on speed."

"This is New York City. If you're that averse to crowds, I've got news for you."

"I wasn't complaining," he said. "Au contraire. I'm fresh out of disco biscuits."

"Are you talking about college students or speed?"

"Wouldn't you like to know," he said. She could hear the smirk in his voice.

They agreed to meet at seven. She worked for a while on her list of suspects—people who could be potentially hazing her and attacking the others. She didn't have evidence that everything was connected, but she had a gut feeling all the activity could be traced back to one person. On a fresh page in her day planner, she jotted their names down in one column, with notes about each of them in another. What she came up with was . . . nothing. Xavier? Sorry, Sloppy Joe, but ghosts weren't real. Stanley and Cal could be safely crossed out. Same with Agnes, who hadn't set foot in the building since the day Lussi had interviewed. She crossed name after name off the list. Eventually, she laid her pen down and settled into a long winter's nap.

CHAPTER TWENTY-FOUR

On her way to meet Fabien, Lussi took a quick detour to the office to pick up the Bible. Gail wasn't at the front desk, but Lussi could hear someone pecking away at a typewriter upstairs. She took a deep breath in the lobby, staring up at the third floor. Her plan was to get in and get out. A covert operation. The sun had already set, and the shadows cast by the wall lamps would conceal her as she slipped into her office.

Cal emerged from the hall into the third-floor foyer. "Oh, hey, boss," he said with a wave. When he raised his arm, his crutch fell to the side. They both watched it tumble down the spiral stairs like the world's loudest Slinky. It came to a rest on the second-floor landing. "It's okay, I've got another one," he shouted down to Lussi.

She walked up the steps and picked up his wayward crutch. So much for being covert. "What are you still doing here?"

"Trying to make up time from this morning. The funeral was really long."

"Catholic service?"

His brow jumped. "How'd you know?"

"Lucky guess," she said. She was about to tell him that since he was an unpaid intern, "making up time" was a moot point. But she'd hold her tongue for now. She had more important matters. She offered to help him down the stairs but wasn't surprised when he declined. Definitely a try-hard if she'd ever met one.

She went to her office and opened the top drawer of her desk. It was empty. Frederick's Bible was missing.

She heard a light knock and glanced up to see Rachael standing in the doorway, silhouetted by the hallway lights. Lussi glanced at her watch; twenty past six. She had to be at Union Square Station in fifteen minutes if she wanted to get to the New York Public Library in time. "Hey, Rachael. I need to head out in a minute. Anything I can help you with?"

Rachael had been to St. Vincent's to see Stanley. His wife wanted to pass along her thanks to Lussi. "Another hour or two and the hemorrhaging in his brain would have killed him."

Lussi placed her hands over her heart. "That's a relief. How soon will he get out? I might stop by to see him."

"He'll be in there for a while. Like, a really, really long while."

Rachael explained that the pencil had drilled deep into the soft tissue of his frontal lobe. Three-quarters of an inch. It didn't sound like much to Lussi, but it was enough to cripple his ability to speak. He could understand you—you could tell by the knowing look in his eyes. He couldn't verbalize his thoughts, though. He couldn't tell you his name or where he was born. He couldn't tell you that Bush was vice president. Every answer was there. Every answer, on the tip of his tongue. Just out of reach.

"He can't even write. There's only one thing he can do," Rachael said. "Draw pictures. And none of them make any sense." She reached into her slacks and unfolded a scrap of notebook paper. "This is the one he gave me. What am I supposed to do, stick it on my fridge?"

Lussi looked it over. The horns, the fur . . . the teeth. He'd sketched Perky. Was this because he'd been in his office staring at the doll all night as he bled out?

Lussi handed the paper back. "Do they know how the accident happened?"

Rachael motioned for Lussi to draw nearer. "You didn't hear this from me, but they're saying it was a suicide attempt," the designer whispered in her ear.

—*stick it where the sun don't shine*—

Lussi glanced out of the corner of her eye at the doll, perched on her bookshelf, thin legs dangling off the edge. Rachael obviously hadn't seen the doll yet, but she would. It was unmistakably the four-horned creature in Stanley's drawing. This would invite questions . . . questions that Lussi didn't know the answer to. Who had gifted her the doll, and for what purpose? The idea of her Secret Santa being a prankster seemed less and less likely by the hour. There was evil in this building. Whether it was Xavier Blackwood's ghost or something else was up for debate. All Lussi knew was that Frederick hadn't been exaggerating when he said she was in danger. She could have easily fallen victim to the slush pile instead of Cal; Stanley could have turned his rage on her instead of on himself. Had Perky been protecting her all this time? Was its magic real?

—*do not bring detestable things into your home*—

There was a loud ping at the window. The blinds were drawn shut, so she couldn't see what had hit it.

Another ping, this time louder.

"Snowballs," Rachael said. "The kids run wild in this neighborhood. A bunch of animals. All from divorced homes, of course. That's how those people live."

Lussi's field of vision was shrinking, the wallpapered walls closing in around her. More pings against the windowpane, one after another after another. Faster. Faster. Faster.

"What . . . what are you talking about?" she asked. "What people?"

"Oh, you know," Rachael said, marching to the window. The barrage was so loud now, it sounded like the building was under attack. "You just have to bang on the window and they run. Watch this."

Rachael yanked on the cord, sending the blinds shooting up. Lussi couldn't see past her reflection, but Rachael was close enough to see through the windowpane. Suddenly, she began to scream long and loud, with the pitch and vibrato of a castrated Luciano Pavarotti. When her voice gave out, she crumpled to the floor.

Lussi rushed over to Rachael to find she had fainted dead away. The pinging came to an abrupt halt. Lussi crouched and slowly peered through the window, just over the sill, dreading the sight of whatever had made Rachael collapse.

The window was plastered with blood-streaked feathers, illuminated from behind by the streetlights. A stained-glass window in the devil's church.

Lussi's nostrils burned with a thick, cloying sweetness. Lavender? Not Rachael's perfume. The fragrance enveloped her, overwhelming her senses. *Okay, I go night night now . . .* she thought as she drifted off into a deep sleep.

CHAPTER TWENTY-FIVE

When Lussi came to, she was on her back staring at an unfamiliar checkerboard ceiling. Her temples were pounding. She lifted the back of her head an inch. It took an outsized amount of effort to complete this simple action. She wasn't on the floor. *A bed?* Too hard. *A table.* It took a few moments for her eyesight to adjust to the dim light, but once it did she could pick out the detail in the wallpaper. *Fleur-de-lis.* She was in the second-floor conference room.

Lussi tried to sit up, but was met with pressure in her chest. Something was holding her down. She craned her head farther upright, pushing her chin as far as she could until it pressed into her clavicle. Her arms and legs were bound tightly to her body with multicolored Christmas lights. Looked like several strands' worth. Dozens of bell-shaped ornaments dangled off the cords.

Somebody had tied Lussi to the conference table with fucking Christmas lights.

The more she struggled, the tighter the strands constricted. After several attempts, she was forced to stop fighting. Her inhales and exhales were growing quick and shallow. She couldn't open her mouth to draw in a deeper breath, or shout for help for that matter. It was taped shut—packing tape, probably. Publishing houses were lousy with packing tape.

You can't pass out again, she told herself. *Steady your breathing.* She'd been knocked out. Drugged. The sweet smell was still present. It was so strong she could taste it. Not lavender . . . chloroform. She'd never smelled it before in her life, but images were coming back to her—the wet rag, the hand pressing it over her mouth and nose as she gasped for air . . .

This was going to make for one fascinating OSHA report.

Shapes were moving at the edges of her vision. Dark figures. Cloaked figures. The fabric shifted as they slunk about, slowly, silently. Gathering around the conference table. The chairs had been wheeled out of the room. She saw less and less wallpaper as their shapeless bodies crowded around her.

". . . who plugged in the Christmas lights . . ."

". . . awake now . . ."

One of the cloaked figures kneeled beside the table, tested the strands of lights. A man. Up close, she could see the stubbled chin underneath his Venetian *Phantom of the Opera* mask. It could have been any one of a dozen of her male coworkers.

Lussi counted six figures total, each in a different plastic Halloween mask. Her coworkers, who'd been conspiring against her all along. It wasn't paranoia, either. Paranoia wasn't even an option, not when you've been chloroformed and tied to a conference table.

Blackwood-Patterson wasn't merely a cult of personality built around Xavier Blackwood.

Blackwood-Patterson was a literal cult.

Because of course it was. The signs were all there: Slavish devotion to their leader. Elitist thinking. Irrational fear of the outside world. Treating the excommunicated like they were dead. Lussi hadn't realized it earlier because none of them had that faraway look in the eyes. The look those Jonestown converts had. The one that signaled nobody was home upstairs.

And yet here they were.

She shivered. The temperature had dropped several degrees in the room since she'd come to. Had someone cracked the door to the fire escape? Lussi's winter jacket and black turtleneck had both been stripped off, leaving her shivering in a white tank top.

One of the figures, this one in a Wonder Woman mask, produced a serrated Rambo-style knife from their cloak. Lussi's eyes widened. The blade was as long as her forearm. It wasn't a prop. If this had all started out as a prank, it had morphed into something else entirely.

Lussi was supposed to turn thirty in two years. The big "three oh." Her sister was already planning a girls' weekend in Vegas for the two of them. Lussi had never been to Vegas. She hadn't been looking forward to it, frankly, but now it was all she wanted. Her life couldn't end here. It couldn't.

"Jesus Christ, where'd you get that?" someone shouted, their voice muffled by their mask.

"It's a bowie knife," Wonder Woman said. "For the ritual. They sell them at the army surplus store in Union Square."

Lussi had known a couple of "devil worshippers" at her high school. All they'd done was listen to prog rock and smoke dope in the parking lot. They'd scared her a little—mostly by how brain-dead they'd seemed—but they'd never tried to sacrifice her. She wanted to go back and apologize for giving them the cold shoulder.

"This isn't a ritual," another woman hissed from underneath a green witch mask. "It's a spiritual cleansing."

"Then why do you want the knife?" Wonder Woman said.

The Green Witch's voice dropped an octave: "To cut her heart out, of course."

CHAPTER TWENTY-SIX

Lussi wasn't sure what pissed her off more: the fact that her coworkers were preparing to remove her heart, or that they thought she needed a spiritual cleansing in the first place. She wasn't some bratty teenager wanking off with a cross, Regan MacNeil style. Even worse, the "cut the heart out" bit was taken straight from *Satan's Lament*. She scanned the room, trying to make eye contact with someone. Anyone. Just yesterday, she might have been in this very room with some of them discussing next year's fall list. Now they were averting their eyes, doing their best to avoid her silent judgment.

"Let me assure you, this is nothing personal, Ms. Meyer," the Green Witch said. "In fact, many of us fought for you. We took a vote and decided not to take immediate action. That was a mistake, as Stanley found out. It's only by God's grace that we stopped you from harming Rachael."

The way the witch said her name, so formal and odd . . . like Mary Beth Wilkerson. But it couldn't be The Raven. If she had a problem with Lussi, she'd confront her. Mano a mano. Wouldn't she?

The Phantom produced a book from his cloak. Frederick's Bible.

"This was found in your imitation Coach bag," the Green Witch said, showing it to the room like evidence in a murder trial. "Doing a little opposition research, are you?" She pulled a folded notebook page from the book. "Oh, and what's this? Looks like a list of your coworkers. There seem to be a few names crossed off . . . Stanley, Xavier . . ."

Lussi struggled against her restraints, shaking her head no, no, no, no. This was a sham trial. They were trying to do her dirty, like the Count of Monte Cristo.

The Green Witch chuckled at Lussi's distress. "Don't hurt yourself, dear," the woman said. "That's our job. Oh, and one last item, before we start: we also found your witch's familiar. Let Alan in."

Alan cut through the mass of cloaked bodies in denim over-alls and a conductor's cap. Just your average sixtysomething maintenance man, toting a plastic cat carrier.

She thrashed on the table and growled from her throat, her screams trapped beneath the tape across her mouth. Alan glanced down at her but didn't look surprised. He looked bored. Like how dare she waste his time by trying to get him involved.

"You brought the creature?" the Green Witch asked.

He raised the cat carrier so everyone could see. Inside, through the carrier's wire door, red eyes burned like hot coals. A trick of the light . . . or something more? The carrier shook, and Alan thwapped it hard. Whatever was inside stopped moving. Was this the animal that had been leaving little treats all over the office?

"Y'all good?" Alan asked. His nonchalance and two-pack-a-day voice reminded Lussi of a Coney Island carnie. The Green Witch dismissed him and he left the carrier behind on the floor.

The Green Witch crossed her arms. "So what do you have to say for yourself, Ms. Meyer? We're all waiting."

Lussi tried again to make some sound resembling speech, without any success.

"Tape," the Green Witch said, pushing another cloaked figure toward the table. The figure—a woman who didn't spend much time on a typewriter, from the looks of her alternating green and red nails—grasped one side of the packing tape. The woman whispered a quiet "sorry" and, without any further warning, gave the tape a hard yank. The sound of it peeling away engulfed the silence in the room.

Lussi gulped for air. The skin around her lips was raw. "I'm not a witch," she said between deep breaths. Her throat was dry, her voice scratched as an old record. "You're making a mistake."

The Green Witch waved her hand around the room theatrically. "Hear how the devil alters her voice!"

Lussi cleared her throat and spat to the side of the table. She could taste copper on her tongue. "So where's your priest? You can't perform a spiritual cleansing without religious supervision."

A figure in a William Shatner *Star Trek* mask raised a hand. "I'm a minister in the Universal Life Church," the man said.

A mail-order priest? Jesus H. Christ on a Popsicle stick.

"You seem to know a lot about this stuff," the Green Witch said to Lussi. Nods all around. Lussi wanted to pull her own hair out, but of course she couldn't move her arms.

"Your little spiritual cleansing exercise is from *Satan's Lament*. A book I edited."

"That was yours?" someone said.

"Also, I'm not the one wearing a witch mask," she said. "So think about that before you start throwing accusations around. Now, if you could untie me, I would super appreciate it. I'm begging you, pretty fucking please, with a cock-sucking titty-fucking popped cherry on top, let me go."

Lussi felt her face flush with embarrassment. She wasn't sure where the words had come from or how her tongue had put them in that order.

"Such vile language," the Green Witch said. "What else would you expect from one who edits filth?"

That sounded like a quote from her mother. She tried not to let on how close the words cut her. "Listen," Lussi said, exasperated, "I don't know why you'd accuse me of being a witch, but I haven't done anything wrong."

"Care to explain your meeting with Frederick Munson?"

Gasps around the room.

"A select few of us received word of said meeting from a reliable source," the Green Witch said. Had they been spying on her? "Did he mention to you that when he was fired, he had to be escorted out of this building in a straitjacket?" Lussi didn't respond. "No, I wouldn't imagine he did. What about going off his meds two months ago, right before he stopped showing up to work? His boss at Random House was most relieved to hear we'd found him."

Lussi didn't want to believe any of it, but what reason did they have to lie? Whatever they told her, she would be taking it to the grave. If Frederick was as batshit crazy as they were implying, had he somehow infected Lussi with his madness? The birds hurling themselves against her office window . . . had that even happened? Was any of this happening?

The Green Witch continued: "His family picked him up this afternoon. Right about now, I'd say they're an hour or two away from the funny farm in upstate New York. The irony, of course, is that all his ranting about an evil presence in this building seems eerily prescient, now that you're here. Oh well." She held out her hand. "Knife, please."

Lussi twisted, trying to wriggle free. They were actually going to go through with this. If it wasn't a ritual sacrifice, it sure felt like one. How much blood, she wondered, had been spilled in this building over the years? How much would have to be spilled until whatever dark force that ruled over it was finally satisfied?

"I don't know what I've done, but I'm sorry," Lussi said. "*Satan's Lament* was fiction, for chrissakes!"

"You don't know what you've done?" the Green Witch said. "You would lie about that today, of all days? The nerve. A legend was buried today, and you act like you don't know what this is all about. You were in the room when Xavier Blackwood had his fatal heart attack . . . without which you wouldn't have a job here. You also told your intern you would break his legs the next time he put them on your desk . . ."

"I did? I don't remember . . ."

"That poor young man remembers," the Green Witch said. "You know what happened next—he kicked his feet up on your desk in the afternoon, when you weren't around. A force of habit. He was scared half to death you would fire him. But the punishment was worse than he could have ever imagined. A few hours later, his shin snapped in two like a twig. Because of *you*."

Lussi shook her head frantically. "How could I have known? You just said so yourself—I wasn't around."

"That's why you have a familiar," the Green Witch said, a smile in her voice that Lussi couldn't see but knew was there. "And then there's Stanley . . . sad, sad Stanley."

Maybe it was just her panic-stricken brain, but what the Green Witch was saying . . . sort of made sense? Lussi *had* said those things. She had no supernatural abilities that she knew of, but those were her words. In the deepest, darkest recesses of her soul, Lussi knew she wasn't capable of hurting anyone. She was a pacifist. She'd marched against the Vietnam War with her parents as a little girl. She'd voted to put a peanut farmer in the White House, of all things. She would never hurt somebody. Not intentionally.

"If you believe I'm capable of doing all of these horrible things," she said, "then what's to stop me from using my dark magic to curse all of you right now? All I need to do is say the words . . ."

The Green Witch polished the blade of the knife with the sleeve of her cloak. "The bells on the strands of light binding you are cast-iron," she said. "Your magic has been nullified. Besides, if you could use your powers to save yourself, you would have by now."

"Counterargument," Lussi said. "I don't have powers, and you all need to reread *The Ox-Bow Incident*."

"Counter-counterargument," the Green Witch said. "The movie was actually better than the book, and also: shut up." She traced the tip of the blade from Lussi's ear to the bottom of her chin. The cold steel made Lussi shiver all over again. She thought of her parents, her sister. Her niece. Her dearly departed Oma.

"The stollen," Lussi said.

The Green Witch stopped what she was doing.

"My fruitcake," Lussi said excitedly. "I brought it in last Monday and somebody took it from the fridge. If there's anybody around here I actually wanted to hurt, it would have been that person. Sloppy Joe was there. He heard me. I said, 'I hope whoever took my fruitcake chokes on it.'"

The room was silent. If Sloppy Joe was among the cloaked figures, he wasn't coming forward.

The Green Witch poked the tip of the knife into her sternum. "You didn't know who took it, so you couldn't work your juju. Since you're not a threat any longer . . ." She leaned in and lifted the bottom of her mask. Lussi felt her hot breath on her ear. "I had the munchies last week," The Raven said with a giggle. "You could have made a lot of friends around here with baking skills like that. Alas."

Lussi had been right about the ringleader. She just hadn't wanted to believe it. She couldn't believe it. There was no question, though. No question at all. The identities of the other participants in this sham were still unknown to her, but Lussi guessed there was at least one side-ponytail underneath those cloaks.

The Raven, standing tall, fit her mask back over her chin. She raised the bowie knife in front of her, locking her elbows. The business end of the knife pointed down at Lussi's heart. Lussi sucked in a great gulp of air and held it, as if doing so could somehow stretch out the moment, her final moment among the living.

The Raven cocked her head to the side. What was she waiting on?

Suddenly, the knife slipped through The Raven's hands, dropping to the floor. The Raven pressed a hand to her own neck, her eyes widening. She waved around frantically for help. All of this happened in silence, like some bizarre pantomime. By the time the others in the room caught on that their de facto leader was choking, The Raven was already dead. Her body tipped forward in slow motion. Her forehead bounced off the edge of the table with a wet smack, and she crumpled to a cloaked heap on the floor.

"The iron," someone said. "It didn't work. What does that mean?"

That's when the Christmas lights cut out, and Lussi's world once again plunged into darkness.

CHAPTER TWENTY-SEVEN

Lussi's tormentors fumbled around in the darkness. She heard them bumping heads and elbowing each other. They were running in circles, blind as Stevie Wonder. The pandemonium wouldn't last forever—if they couldn't find the light switch for the wall sconces, somebody would draw the shades up. Lussi had to take advantage of their temporary confusion and escape.

With a snap, the strands of Christmas lights holding Lussi down went slack. She could move again. Somebody had cut her loose. Something was pressed into her right hand. The knife. Someone curled her fingers around the handle for her. So she had an ally in the room after all.

No time for questions. She secured the knife and rolled off the table, landing hard on her hip. She held the knife blade down like she'd seen Special Forces do in the movies. Less likely to accidentally stab someone. She wanted to defend herself, not add to her (alleged) body count.

Lussi felt along the wall for the door. Her fingers met the windowpane. In all the confusion, she'd rolled off the wrong side of the table. Someone bumped into her, sending her stumbling. She landed on top of The Raven's corpse, causing a pulpy liquid to ooze out of the former editor in chief's mouth.

Lussi detected notes of cardamom and brandy.

Oma's fruitcake?

How is this even possible? she asked herself. Someone—or something—had caused Blackwood-Patterson's editor in chief to choke on a fruitcake that had to have passed through her digestive tract a week ago. Lussi was no witch, but maybe some supernatural force really was working in her favor.

She needed to get out of here. She needed time to think. But also, she was forgetting something . . .

The cat carrier! Of course. Had there really been glowing red eyes emanating from within? She couldn't leave without taking another look. Maybe it was a raccoon after all—"Cyndi Lauper," as Digby had called the pest running loose in the building. But maybe it was something else.

She army-crawled under the table, searching blindly with her hands until her fingers met the cold, hard plastic. The carrier was tipped on its side. Somebody must have accidentally booted it. She felt for the door. It was unlatched. She reached inside, ready to withdraw her fingers if something snapped at her. The last thing she wanted was a series of rabies shots. Not with the month she was having.

Empty. Whatever it was had taken off.

A light was flickering in the hallway. Somebody had found a candle. Time was running out. She wanted to prove her innocence, but now wasn't the time. Especially since she was beginning to question her role in what was happening herself.

Lussi lunged for the door, hurtling herself through several of her coworkers and sending them flying like bowling pins. She made it to the hallway and ran through another cloaked coworker, knocking them over, then flew down the stairs, taking the steps two, three at a time, ignoring the shouts behind her. The lobby was dimly lit by the streetlights filtering in. She skidded to a stop on the linoleum before reaching the door, her Keds squeaking.

Footsteps on the stairs behind her.

"C'mon, c'mon, c'mon," she muttered, fumbling with the locks.

Footsteps on tile, getting closer.

She turned the final deadbolt and pulled the door open. A great gust swept into the building, along with a dusting of snow. A yellow cab was parked directly out front. The light on top indicated it was available. The likelihood of a cab picking up a fare in this neighborhood after dark was remote. This was the most compelling evidence of a supernatural force at work so far.

Lussi pulled the heavy door shut behind her. She skated across the ice-covered sidewalk toward the curb. Just as she reached the taxi, the rear passenger door swung open. Behind her, she heard the building's great iron door do the same.

No time for pleasantries. Lussi dumped herself into the backseat ass-first, pushing a bundled-up passenger across the ripped vinyl bench seat, and pulled the door closed. "Drive," she said, banging on the bullet-proof partition to get the cabbie's attention. "Anywhere, I don't care, just drive!"

The cabbie, who'd been fiddling with his meter, glanced at her in the rearview mirror. He looked like the kid in *Indiana Jones*. He might have just gotten his cab medallion yesterday. Hell, he might have just gotten his license yesterday.

"She's with me," an unmistakably familiar British voice said. Fabien carefully disarmed her of the knife, which she hadn't realized she still had clutched in her hand. "Hundred Fourteenth and Broadway," he told the driver. "Five bucks for every red light you run . . . and another twenty to not ask any questions."

The driver looked to the Blackwood Building. Lussi didn't see anyone but she knew her cloaked coworkers were lurking behind the cracked door, dark forms of shifting shape and mass. Either they were afraid to test the outside steps—slick-bottomed dress shoes and heels weren't exactly all-terrain footwear—or they didn't want to expose themselves to potential witnesses.

"Ten bucks a red," the cabbie said, starting the meter, "and keep the twenty. I don't want to know a damn thing." He pulled a wide U-turn across four lanes of honking traffic, and just like that Lussi and Fabien Nightingale were headed uptown.

CHAPTER TWENTY-EIGHT

Fabien's Harlem apartment was small but resplendent with old-world charm. In his fireplace, a fire roared, which he occasionally tended to. Lussi was wrapped up in a cocoon of half a dozen fleece blankets in a tall-backed reading chair. A pretty, doe-eyed woman brought in two cups of floral tea and then left without a word.

"Nice place you've got here," Lussi said, blowing on her tea. In all the years they'd known each other, they'd never actually met at his house. Always at her office, or a nearby bar. Usually a bar. "Was that your housekeeper?"

"My mother," he said.

"She staying with you over the holidays?"

"And beyond," he said wearily. "It's her apartment."

Lussi raised a brow. "Is this a Norman Bates situation?"

He scoffed. "You've seen my royalty statements. Do you really think I could live in the city—even across One Hundred and Tenth Street—on what I make?"

"I suppose not," she said, feeling guilty for having broached the subject. She didn't like to make inquiries into her authors' lives. She preferred to think they were independently wealthy. An inheritance, maybe. Either that, or involved in some sort of top-dollar sex work.

Lussi caught him up on everything—not just what had happened tonight, but everything from the past week she'd been holding off on telling him. It felt good to get it all out in the open, even if some of it felt silly once she'd said it aloud. He listened without interjection, hands clasped, tap-tap-tapping his index fingers together. "If you hadn't come looking for me, they might have chased me down," she said. "I wouldn't be here right now; I'd be a chalk outline in the East Village. If they can make chalk outlines on ice."

He nodded. "I waited for an hour and a half at the library. You never struck me as the type to ditch without a word, so I called your offices from a pay phone. The main number, whatever's in the phone book. No answer, not even a machine to leave messages." He looked over the red indentations on her wrists. "We should get pictures of these before they fade."

"What good would it do? I didn't see anyone's face, except for Alan's." She sunk into the chair. "We can't involve the police. They're liable to toss me in the loony bin with Frederick, regardless of the evidence."

Fabien set down his tea. "Here's the good news: you're most definitely not a murderer. You can't be convicted in a court of law for a few tossed-off comments. How were you to know somebody would take them as literal orders? You're also not a witch. I've known many witches, and they all smelled like patchouli."

"What do I smell like?" she asked.

"At the moment? I'd rather not say."

"Thanks for the vote of confidence. I think."

"As far as this Bible you were given . . ."

Lussi could only shake her head. "They took it from me. I'd

kept it at the office because Frederick warned me not to take it home. That it was 'detestable.'"

"'Do not bring detestable things into your home, for then you will be destroyed, just like them,'" Fabien said, reciting what Frederick had said word for word. "Deuteronomy 7:26."

A Bible verse. If only she'd ever cracked the Bible her mother had given her, she might have recognized it. "He wasn't warning me not to take it home," she said, realization dawning on her. "He was warning me about . . . something else. Something already in the building. Something detestable. The source of this 'evil' he felt."

"Perhaps."

"You don't sound convinced."

"If what they told you about Frederick checks out, we can rent a car. Head upstate to this mental facility. Talk our way in, compare notes with him. I do have to warn you, the bit about him being bonkers? It may be true."

"If he's nuts, then so am I. I saw something move in that cat carrier. It could've been a raccoon, or even some benign house pet, but the birds—the birds flying into the window to their deaths—were real. Whatever is at work here, it's evil."

"I'm not dismissing anything outright, I'm simply urging caution," he said. "Have you heard of the Meowing Nuns?"

"Is that a punk band?"

Fabien crossed the living room to the fireplace. "This happened in the Middle Ages. France." He lifted a white-tailed deer head off its hook on the wall. "A single nun began meowing like a cat one day, apparently having lost her ability to speak. Other nuns joined her, one by one, until the entire convent was infected. They meowed for hours on end, unable to stop."

"Sounds annoying," Lussi said.

"Indeed. Soldiers were called in to quell the outbreak." There was a safe inside the wall where the deer head had been. Fabien spun the dial. "During the Middle Ages, cats were seen as emissaries of the devil. The nuns believed themselves to be possessed by Satan."

Fabien withdrew a plastic bag from the safe. "Today, we recognize it as a case of mass hysteria," he continued, speaking over the crackling fire. "Delusions are as contagious as viruses. They can replicate in populations in a similar manner."

Lussi stared at him in silence. He didn't believe her. And why should he? Even she was beginning to doubt herself. With every passing minute, what had happened in the Blackwood Building seemed more like a bad dream.

Fabien's mother returned, dutifully refilling their tea. "You must be so proud of your son," Lussi said, ignoring Fabien's scowl. "He's quite the author."

The woman looked her son up and down. Her features softened. "He's very talented," she said, "but he's no Stephen King."

Fabien waited for his mother to leave, then settled back into his chair. He turned to Lussi. "You know, I don't think you're the first one this has happened to."

"The first one to try to make conversation with your mother?"

"The first new hire or intern Blackwood-Patterson has done this sort of thing to. Remember when I told you I'd heard stories about Xavier Blackwood? I'm beginning to think that wasn't idle gossip."

"I assumed you meant he was just a typical creepy boss."

"That he may have been, but the rumors were of a more sinister variety. A friend of mine teaches at Columbia. Apparently, Blackwood-Patterson has been restricted from participating in their internship program. There were a number of . . . disappearances. From different universities, mind you. I'm not sure if police reports were ever filed—you know how flighty college students can be. They probably assumed the kids had returned home to Boise, Idaho." He shuddered. "I'd rather disappear."

Lussi had never heard the rumors, but she could believe it. Her coworkers had seemed quite surprised to see Cal. It made sense now why Digby had pulled him from a film department—the whisper network didn't extend outside the English and creative writing programs. This also meant the "accidents" inside the Black-wood Building pre-dated Lussi. Cold comfort, however. Especially for poor Cal. For all she knew, he could be trapped in the building with those psychopaths. Unless he was in on it. He'd been in the secret meeting . . .

Fabien shook two round, pale blue pills out of the baggie. Knowing him, they weren't ibuprofen. "What do you have there?" she asked.

"You're never going to get to sleep on your own," he said. "And you'll be totally useless tomorrow if you don't get some shut-eye. I thought maybe you could use some friends, to help you count sheep. They'll dissolve in your tea. No hangover, I promise."

"How long do they take to kick in? I don't want to fall into a coma on the express train."

"Mum is making up the guest room for you right now. You can't go back to your apartment until this is all resolved. They may be waiting there to finish what they started."

"I wasn't talking about going to Staten Island," she said. "I need to go back to the office. My handbag is there. Everything's in it—my wallet, my ID. The last of my cash, until Friday."

"Your coworkers tried to cut out your still-beating heart."

"Only six of them. And one's dead now."

"It's a suicide mission," Fabien said.

She waved him off. "If I walk in through the front door, sure.

But they're always cracking the door to the fire escape and forgetting about it."

"The heating bill must be outrageous," Fabien said, shaking his head in wonder. "You're not thinking about retrieving anything else from the building, I hope?"

The thought of grabbing the Percht had crossed her mind. Without it, she was vulnerable to evil spirits, which . . . she didn't believe in? Her mind was split between two worlds. She looked away.

He set the blue pills on the end table between them.

The faint sound of a jazz trumpet reached them from a room down the hall. The *Charlie Brown Christmas* soundtrack. Fabien returned the plastic bag to the wall safe. "You'd better like Christmas jazz," he said over his shoulder. "That's all Mum plays this time of year. And the rest of the year, for that matter. Not the easiest conditions in which to write a horror novel."

His book. She'd completely forgotten about it. He hadn't asked once for her thoughts on *Transylvanian Dirt*, though he'd surely been dying to. Authors were among God's neediest creatures, eclipsed only by actors and puppies. His restraint and selflessness in the face of what she'd been through were the marks of true friendship. It made her realize she couldn't ask him to follow her down this road. Setting foot inside the Blackwood Building again was a suicide mission. She knew Fabien was right—everything was replaceable—but she also knew whatever this was wasn't over. The Raven was dead. Someone had killed her. And Lussi needed to know who—or what.

While Fabien carefully remounted the deer head above the fireplace, Lussi leaned over the end table and dropped the pills into his tea.

And then she waited.

CHAPTER TWENTY-NINE

Agnes Bailey answered the door after one ring of the bell, as if she'd been sitting close by, waiting for Lussi to arrive on her doorstep. Lussi was surprised—it was a quarter to midnight—but then checked herself. She was only a few hours removed from nearly having her heart cut out in a conference room. Nothing should have surprised her at this point.

The old woman was dressed in a royal-purple terrycloth bathrobe. Smile lines tugged at the edges of her eyes. Her hair was stark white. It was difficult to believe this was the hussy who'd stolen Xavier Blackwood from Digby's mother. Even more difficult to believe this was the woman who'd been in charge of the intern program . . . a program that had, either directly or indirectly, resulted in an untold number of missing coeds.

Lussi introduced herself. Agnes only nodded, inviting her in without a word. No surprise, no *what are you doing here*. Mr. Blackwood's former secretary was playing the part of a fugitive who'd been cornered, a woman tired of running. Apparently her guilty conscience wasn't letting her sleep.

The aroma of baking bread permeated the house. Lussi stomped the snow off her tennis shoes inside the entryway but kept her coat on. It was Fabien's gray fur—gargantuan on her frame, but perfect for concealing the bowie knife she'd hidden in its inside pocket.

Lussi followed Agnes into the kitchen. The Long Island ranch-style home was simple and unpretentious, with orange wallpaper that had been dated the moment it was put up. Hadn't been difficult to find—there were several Agnes Baileys in the phone book, but only one in Massapequa, the town Lussi recalled Digby mentioning. Hard name to forget. The woman's house was spacious compared to city dwellings, but far from the "palatial estate" Digby had described. The suburban backyard was lit by an alley street-light. Snow covered the lawn. It could have been a Christmas card, if not for the elevated LIRR tracks just beyond the fence line.

Agnes went to the cupboard next to the stove. "You look like you could use a coffee. I've got Vienna roast, Suisse Mocha . . ."

"Anything without sugar," Lussi said. She took a seat at the dining room table, draping her coat over the chair back. This room was several degrees warmer due to the oven.

"NutraSweet okay?" Agnes asked.

"Just black coffee for me, thanks."

Agnes spooned the instant coffee mix from a red-and-orange tin. If Lussi had learned anything from Shirley Jackson, it was to be wary of condiments in the homes of strangers. The polite act was a put-on. Agnes was not simply Xavier's secretary or personal assistant. She was the keeper of his secrets. His misdeeds. How much had she covered up for him?

Agnes sat across the table. The skin on her forearms was loose and hung like clothes on a line. She poured a dollop of creamer into her own coffee and stirred it. She pushed the creamer pitcher to the center of the table.

Lussi did not touch it.

Agnes stared into her mug for five minutes. Ten minutes. Just the two of them, sitting in silence. Agnes was clearly engrossed in whatever was happening in her coffee. It was as if she were trying to divine the future. Finally, she looked up at Lussi.

Tears welled in her eyes.

Lussi reached for Agnes's hand—instinct, nothing more—but the woman withdrew it and raised her mug to her lips. She was an old woman who was done with comfort, who didn't need pity from a twenty-eight-year-old girl who knew nothing about life.

"I'm sorry for your loss," Lussi said. She found her desire for answers conflicting with her innate compassion. This woman had buried her partner only that morning. "I couldn't attend the services. I'm sorry."

Agnes's face softened. "I wasn't there, either. Emotions tend to run high at funerals, in my experience. Why complicate things?"

"Because you loved him?"

"I did, you know. Love him. His ex-wife never forgave us— she still thinks I'm the Antichrist. The Church wouldn't marry us. They're old fashioned about that sort of thing. So in a way I suppose I did take him down a dark path. I assure you our relationship wasn't as tawdry as it sounds. Secretary, boss . . . you know how that is. It's not like we were locking his door and making love every day over lunch hour." She smiled at the memory. "Not *every* day, at least."

Lussi about choked on her coffee.

"Watch out, it's a little hot, Laura," Agnes said.

"Lussi."

"Of course. Lussi," the woman said. "You didn't come all the way here to listen to an old lady reminisce about her affairs over instant coffee. You're here because you've got boy trouble."

"Boy trouble?"

Agnes smiled. "Sorry, force of habit. He's thirty-five, but he'll always be a boy to me."

"I'm sorry, who's thirty-five?"

"Why, Digby, of course. Thought I'd heard you two were an item?" The oven's buzzer went off, loud and harsh. "That would be the fruitcake. I'll be right back."

———

Lussi felt like hammering her forehead into the table. Repeatedly. How could she have been so clueless? She was twenty-eight, a rising star in the world of genre fiction. Compared to the aging workforce at the Blackwood Building, though, Lussi was barely legal. She had talked herself into a senior position—unheard of for somebody her age, even with her experience. No wonder rumors had been circulating about her and the new boss.

"Could I use your restroom?" Lussi asked. Agnes, pulling the fruitcake from the oven, pointed her down the hall.

Lussi found it and flipped the light switch. The toilet seat was padded. *Where do old ladies find these things?* she wondered, sitting down.

She had to remind herself why she was here. Frederick had told her about a long list of injuries and disappearances—the missing interns from Fabien's story. *Dead kids, call them what they are, dead kids*, she chided herself. She could hardly believe it would go unnoticed amongst the staff. If interns had been disappearing from Blackwood-Patterson for years, her coworkers had to know. Agnes might have been in charge of the internship program, but she wasn't the only one guilty here. Were the intern deaths a warning to staff, perhaps? Was it why people never left the company, for fear that some smiting spirit would come after them? It almost came together for her, except Frederick—Frederick had escaped with his life.

She reached for the toilet paper, but the roll was bare. Awesome. The hits kept coming. Lussi nosed around the sides of the toilet for a crocheted TP holder. Nada. She twisted to look behind her and found a wooden box on top of the tank. An antique, from the looks of the flaking black paint. She was about to flip the lid when she paused. It wasn't any old box. It was the box from Mr. Blackwood's shelf. The one he'd kept the Percht in . . . the one with the iron clasp and hinges.

CHAPTER THIRTY

Toilet paper—two spare rolls. That was all that was inside the box in Agnes's bathroom, thank God. As Lussi replaced the empty tube with a fresh roll, she tried to imagine how the box had wound up in Agnes's home. According to Digby, his father's secretary had walked out the day of Lussi's interview and never come back. Not even to clear out her desk. But Agnes had taken something with her, after all. Which she was now using to store double-ply.

Lussi scrubbed her hands. Did this mean that the woman was her Secret Santa? If she'd meant to protect Lussi from evil, why hadn't she come clean already? That wasn't all, though. The timing was all wrong. Agnes couldn't have known Lussi was going to be hired by Digby Blackwood at the hospital. It was impossible. Lussi was mulling the question over as she returned to the dining room. There, she found Agnes seated at the table, bowie knife in hand.

The woman looked up at Lussi. "We need to talk, sweetie."

Run. Lussi's first instinct was to get the hell out of here and not look back.

But why? Despite what she may have done in the past, this woman wasn't a threat. Not with a knife, at least. Maybe not even with a gun—Agnes hardly looked like she had the strength to pull a trigger.

Lussi sat across from her. "I saw the box."

"I thought you might," Agnes said. "I'd forgotten all about it— at my age, you forget just about everything except what night *Matlock* is on." She sighed. "I'm disappointed in you, Laura. I thought we were having a nice time, and then I find this knife. Imagine my surprise."

"Somebody attacked me with it."

Agnes shook her head slowly. "The city, it gets more and more violent every year. Especially the East Village. The city needs to take that park back."

"It was Mary Beth," Lussi said. "Not some street psycho, not a mugger. Blackwood-Patterson's editor in chief."

"Can't say I'm surprised. She always did have a mean streak."

"She's dead."

This got Agnes's full attention.

"She choked to death," Lussi clarified. "She's not the only one who has been targeted, either. Stanley's in the hospital. A brain injury. He might never recover. My intern has a broken leg and bruised ribs. More people will be hurt unless I put a stop to this."

"Ah. But you can't stop it, my dear. He's chosen you."

Lussi's blood ran cold. She watched Agnes carefully as the old woman turned the knife in her hands. How much did she really know about this old woman at the end of the day?

"Are you talking about Xavier?" Lussi said, almost in a whisper.

Agnes giggled. "Not Xavier. The boy."

This time, Lussi knew she wasn't referring to Digby.

"How much do you know about the Nazis and the occult?" Agnes said calmly as she used the bowie knife to slice the fruitcake. This conversation was certainly taking a left turn.

"Assume I know nothing," Lussi said.

Agnes plated the fruitcake. "Hitler had a well-documented fascination with the occult. The Third Reich sought out ancient treasures they thought could turn the tide of the war. Obviously, they failed in their pursuit of a supernatural game changer. A weapon is only powerful when it's wielded by someone who knows how to use it." Agnes ran a finger lightly over the blade's edge. "That box is Nazi paraphernalia, discovered by our former employer in the snowy fields of Germany at the close of World War II. But it's not the box that should interest you—it's what's inside. Or what was inside."

The skin of Lussi's forearms pricked with gooseflesh. "The Percht."

Agnes nodded approvingly. "So you're familiar with the legend surrounding your gift."

"My grandmother had one. She told us stories, but nothing I remember. They're like dreams now."

"She didn't have one like this," Agnes said. "This one is special. Within days of discovering it, Xavier's luck turned a sharp corner. Too sharp, perhaps. First he was shipped back to the States months ahead of schedule. Then, when he arrived home, he learned he would soon be newly flush with cash. The price, however, was steep: his parents had died in a car accident less than two weeks earlier. His newfound wealth was a settlement from the automobile company."

"I don't mean to be rude, but I don't need his life story."

Agnes slid a plate and fork across the table to Lussi. "If you don't see the point yet, you're not as smart as I thought you were."

"Don't tell me the Percht killed his parents."

"In a way, yes. I can't say how Xavier knew this. He just sensed a connection to the doll, understood that it was influencing his life. It became more apparent as his wealth began to accumulate. He loved the boy like a son. He needed to hide it away, though—not in a box, but in a fortress."

The Blackwood Building. A four-story brownstone built by a long-dead, superstitious first-generation immigrant.

Lussi sipped her coffee. It was cold.

"Some magic must have inevitably leaked out of the building," Agnes said. "The unnatural scent lured strange folk to the neighborhood, although if you asked them, none would know exactly *why* they were drawn to the area. The Blackwood Building was a freak magnet. It's no coincidence the city's lost souls have made their home in Tompkins Square Park. Look at how the writers and artists, alcoholics and junkies, and just plain crazies have taken over the East Village."

Lussi stabbed the fruitcake with her fork, her patience dwindling. "It sounds to me like Xavier became paranoid and locked himself away in a four-story coffin."

"Believe what you want."

Lussi said nothing.

"It took me weeks to buy into it," Agnes said. "It was all so fantastical. But I saw things that I couldn't deny. It didn't take long for him to realize that the doll would enrich him for life, as long as he catered to his . . . whims. The Perchten, you see, are servants of the one called Frau Perchta. When their chains are broken, however, you can train them to be house spirits and serve a new master."

Lussi's head was swimming with newfound knowledge. The events of the past couple of weeks were finally beginning to make sense. She didn't want to believe it—didn't want to believe a damn word—but the pieces were fitting together too well. There was evil in the building after all. Evil inside the one thing she stupidly thought was there to protect her.

Agnes pointed the tip of the knife at Lussi. "He enjoys the things you make him do. You are his *Frauchen* now—his owner. His mistress. You're the reason he killed my Xavier."

Lussi thought of what The Raven, dressed as the Green Witch, had pointed out to her. Lussi had idly cursed the fruitcake thief, Cal, and Stanley. Look what had happened to them. Except . . .

"I never wished for Xavier to die."

Agnes's fingers curled around the knife handle so tight that her knuckles went white. "Didn't you?"

"I certainly did not!" Lussi shouted. "And I certainly didn't ask to be this doll's master."

"'You wouldn't know a good book if it walked into your office and took a bite out of your cold black heart.' I heard you through the door. Those were your exact words."

"That's not a threat," Lussi said, seething.

"There was so much rage in you then. And there's rage in you now. That's why he chose you. I merely assisted, as I've always done."

"You're my Secret Santa," Lussi said. It wasn't possible, yet it *was.*

"In a sense. The boy guided me. I placed him in a gift box from the basement and left him under the tree before I even knew what I was doing. When I was fully lucid again, I was on the train to Long Island with his wooden box tucked in my handbag. And I knew that I could never go back."

"I don't accept your gift," Lussi said flatly.

"I'm sorry, dear. This is one gift you can't return. Your fortunes have already changed—you said so yourself."

"I never—"

"But you did, child. Mary Beth. Now that she's gone, who do you think will take over her position?"

Lussi's eyes widened. "I would never—"

Agnes shook her head. "You don't realize you already have. And now you must do your part. You must make sure the boy is properly fed."

Lussi didn't even bother to ask. She already knew. *The interns.*

This was too much. Way too much. She pushed herself out from the table. "I'm leaving, and I'm taking that damn box with me," Lussi said. "And then you're going to call the police and turn yourself in. The families of those interns deserve closure."

Agnes didn't say anything. Her eyes were vacant, opaque.

"Agnes?" Lussi said. "Did you hear me? I don't know how involved you were, and I don't want to know. But you are complicit, at the very least, and you must answer for your . . . crimes."

Blood the color of holly berries foamed from the woman's mouth. It formed a slick down her chin, drip drip dripping onto the white lace tablecloth. Lussi reached out but then withdrew her hand as the blood started to come faster, faster, a river now—a great bubbling torrent, spewing forth. Agnes's eyes rolled back, leaving only the whites visible. Her head tipped forward in slow motion, and then, with a quick snap, the brittle, osteoporosis-riddled vertebrae in her neck powdered to dust, leaving her head hanging at an unnatural angle.

There was a clatter on the tile at Agnes's feet. Lussi looked below the table and saw the knife's blood-stained blade glowing in the kitchen light. Blood dripped from the old woman's hands as they dangled lifelessly from her lap.

The old woman had told Lussi all she was willing to tell. She would take Xavier's remaining secrets with her to the grave.

That was what had sealed it for Lussi. She realized she'd been on the fence about what was behind the happenings at Black-wood-Patterson for too long. Denial. That's what it had been. There was no denying it any longer—Lussi had to either give in or go mad.

She gave in.

Xavier Blackwood had said the Percht was no toy. He'd known its power. He'd also made a fatal mistake by believing he could control it. As soon as it was tired of him, the Percht dropped him like a publisher axing an author who'd been caught plagiarizing.

The horror hadn't begun with Lussi . . . but it could end with her.

CHAPTER THIRTY-ONE

Lussi parked Agnes's Yugo around the corner from the Blackwood Building underneath a burned-out streetlight. It was nearly three in the morning. She had never stolen a car before and never planned to again. Tonight was turning out to be a night of many firsts—first time she'd drugged a friend, first time she'd been tied to a conference table, first time she'd become master of a demonic doll.

The drive into the city had been terrifying. She couldn't afford to be pulled over. She'd kept the speedometer well under the speed limit. Not that she could go any faster—every time she approached fifty-five, the Yugo started shaking like it had caught the Holy Spirit. The AM radio only picked up talk this time of night, but it was loud enough to mask the sputtering engine. Larry King's monotone also served to drown out any thoughts she might have had of backing out.

All the pieces had come together as she drove toward the East Village. Her coworkers seemed to understand that there was some sort of supernatural force at work in the building and that it could be bound with iron—hence the bells they'd tried to bind her with. Perhaps they had assumed that Xavier had been protecting them and that, without him, they were at the mercy of the spirit, made flesh in the form of a brand-new senior editor who seemed to be on hand for every maiming and death in the building for weeks now.

And they were right to suspect her. They just didn't have the whole story.

Lussi pulled the Percht's box from the trunk and marched down the street toward the Blackwood Building, her wrists jangling with silver bracelets she'd lifted from Agnes's jewelry box. They weren't iron, but—if nineteenth-century German folklore could be believed—they would offer some modicum of protection.

Every fiber in her body wanted to believe that Agnes was either delusional or an outright liar. But she knew, in her heart, that the woman had told her the truth. A person wouldn't kill herself to protect a lie. If she believed Agnes, she also had to believe that Perky would seek out a new master even if Lussi never set foot in the building again. Someone who wasn't ungrateful. Lussi couldn't afford to wait weeks or even days to box it up and blunt its reign of terror. She only had until the first staffers began to roll in around eight thirty.

A chilling calm had come over the neighborhood. Fabien's coat was plenty warm, as was the sweater she's taken from Agnes's closet, red and embroidered with snowflakes, Christmas trees, presents, and snowmen. There was something creepy about wearing a dead woman's clothing and jewelry, but wasn't that what a lot of thrift store finds were anyway? Plus, Agnes was the one who'd disemboweled herself by performing ritual *hara-kiri*, splattering blood all over Lussi's white tank. What else was she supposed to do?

The park was quiet. An orange glow emanated from its deeper recesses. The blanket merchants had packed up long ago; the panhandlers were resting for the night until the world woke up again tomorrow. Three gutter punks were having a snowball fight in the street. As Lussi passed them on the sidewalk, she could hear their laughter echoing off the surrounding buildings. A taxi swerved around them and kept going, the driver leaning on the horn. The punks flipped him off.

Ah, to be young again.

"Hey, lady," one of them said. A teenaged boy from the look of his pockmarked face. "What's in the box?"

Lussi picked up her pace. She should have parked closer to the office, but she hadn't wanted to try her luck in case anyone was watching for her. She ignored the punks' taunts and turned down the alley that went past the back of the Blackwood Building. The fire escape was still her best bet to get into the building unnoticed.

"We're talkin' to you, little miss rich bitch," another punk said, closer now.

Lussi paused only for a moment to look over her shoulder to see if it was time to kick into high gear. Too late. The three kids had caught up to her, encircling her like a pack of wild dogs. They were close enough that she could smell the whiskey on them.

"I don't have money," Lussi said. Her breath hung in the air.

"I asked what was in the box," the first kid said. He was, like the others, wearing denim from head to toe. His jacket was decorated with hundreds of silver studs. He couldn't have been older than fourteen or fifteen. A runaway. An addict. A troublemaker. All of the above.

"Toilet paper," Lussi said.

"Open it," the third one said, a girl with a shaved head. She had so many piercings on her face that it looked like she'd been in a teleporter accident with a stapler.

Lussi lifted the lid, showing off what was inside.

Not toilet paper.

She'd cleaned most of the blood from the bowie knife except

for some stubborn stains on the handle that refused to come out. The punks scattered, arms and legs pinwheeling. The two boys disappeared around the corner but the girl slipped on a patch of ice, faceplanting on the concrete.

Against her better judgment, Lussi helped her to her feet. The girl's fingerless gloves exposed her frozen fingertips. "You got a winter jacket?" Lussi asked, aware of how much she sounded like her mother now.

The girl shook her head.

"You want this one? It's real fur. Unless you're one of those PETA types."

The girl looked at her skeptically. The sable fur was worth several thousand dollars. It wasn't Lussi's to give away, but Fabien would forgive her. Maybe.

"C'mon," Lussi said, shrugging out of the coat. "I'll trade you. You could buy twenty denim jackets with this if you wanted."

"You're crazy, lady," the girl said. She removed her studded denim jacket. "I like you."

"All the best people are crazy," Lussi said. Maybe that was true, and maybe it wasn't. There was, however, a method to Lussi's madness. She wasn't being altruistic; this wasn't the goodness of Lussi's heart finally coming to light. Lussi was going into battle against an evil that may have been older than the city itself. She needed more than a half dozen jangling bracelets.

She needed armor.

CHAPTER THIRTY-TWO

The ladder to the fire escape stopped about ten feet off the ground. Too high for Lussi to reach, even if she had a pair of Air Jordans. Thankfully, the dumpster was close enough to jump from. She set the wooden box on top and hoisted herself up.

As soon as she stood tall on the dumpster's lid, the plastic began to buckle under her weight. She didn't even have time to curse before it gave way, dropping her straight into the trash. There was just enough garbage to cushion her fall.

She tried to climb out, but the trash was like quicksand—with every step, she sank further into the rotting mass. She touched down on the bottom and wetness seeped into her shoes, pooling between her toes. Dumpster sludge. At least now she could finally get some traction and wade to the edge. She was about to pull herself up onto the rim when the second-floor fire escape door swung open, spilling light into the alley.

Digby stepped out onto the landing and peered over the railing. Lussi could only see his silhouette, but nobody else in the office wore a suit jacket with shoulder pads that big. Had he been in the secret meeting about her the other day? Had he been under one of the cloaks earlier tonight?

"Get out of there, you derelicts. I've got a gun," he shouted, not recognizing her in the dim light. "It's very large."

"It's Lussi," she yelled back. "My door code wasn't working."

She waited to see whether that would stop him from firing a warning shot or cause him to empty the firearm's clip into her. "I don't really have a gun," he said. "Meet me out front and I'll let you in."

He went back inside. More lights flipped on. Lussi could see the trash in Technicolor now. The plastic bags were full of ragged-edged holes. They'd been ripped open by tiny teeth . . . or not-so-tiny teeth. She wasn't going to wait around any longer to find out. As she hoisted herself out, her left foot snagged on something. She looked down to see her foot was caught in an elastic band. It was the plastic green witch mask, wedged between two heavy trash bags. A reminder of what was at stake.

▬

Of all the ways she'd imagined getting back inside the building, simply walking through the front door had never crossed her mind. Lussi had assumed her access code would have been deleted from the security system; or, if it hadn't, that it would alert somebody off-site that she'd returned. The locks were the most high-tech thing about the building—if there were closed-circuit TV cameras watching the entrance or front desk, she'd never seen evidence of them.

Digby held the door open for her. She stepped through with the box. She half expected to burst into flame like Michael Jackson on the set of a Pepsi commercial. When she didn't catch fire, she breathed a silent sigh of relief.

"Interesting jacket," Digby said, locking the door behind her.

He'd flipped the lobby lights on. "Don't think I would have pegged you for a Maiden fan."

She craned her head to look at the patch on her back but couldn't see it without taking the jacket off. Which she wasn't about to do. Since she had no iron, the silver was the only thing shielding her from the Percht.

"Iron Maiden," he clarified.

"My roommate's," she said, glancing around. "So is it just you here, or . . ."

"Alan's probably around, but good luck finding him." Digby rubbed his eyes. "Couldn't sleep. Long day, burying Dad. Thought I'd come do some work. Walked in the door and heard the ruckus out back."

"I wanted to be at the service but something came up. I'm sorry."

He narrowed his bloodshot eyes at her. The collar on his wrinkled white polo was popped. It didn't look hip on him; it looked tired. Dated. She could smell his cologne—Obsession for Men. Must have been using it to cover up the fact that he hadn't showered in days. Weeks, possibly. They were both hiding something, and they both knew that the other knew. She wanted to be the first to come clean, to get everything off her chest.

"I have something to tell you," they both said at the same time.

He laughed. "Jinx."

"Really?"

He playfully slugged her upper arm. "Buy me a Diet Rite, and I'll lift it."

"I don't have time for this," she said.

He hit her again and smirked. "I could do this alllllll night."

She glared at him. Now was not the time to push her buttons. She hadn't been up this late since college. Her socks were soaked through with garbage juice. The last time she'd had anything to eat was over twelve hours ago—her blood sugar had to be out of whack. Oh, and there was the tiny matter of the Nazi devil doll roaming the halls of the Blackwood Building.

But sure, she had time to get Digby a pop from the break room. Who did this guy think he was?

Your boss, dodo brain, she reminded herself. The one everyone apparently thinks you're sleeping with. No wonder they were so quick to villainize her.

"Fine. I'll bring it up in ten. I need to clean up first. I'm sure I smell wonderful."

He cocked his head to one side, possibly contemplating whether she'd broken the jinx code. He decided to let it slide. "Diet Rite. None of that RC crapola," he said, snapping his fingers and pointing at her.

He mounted the winding staircase. When he reached the fourth floor and disappeared from sight, Lussi rushed to Gail's desk and opened the top drawer.

The gun was missing.

CHAPTER THIRTY-THREE

On her way to the vending machines, Lussi stopped at the conference room doorway. There was no sign she'd ever been held captive here—no cut-up strands of Christmas lights, no tipped-over cat carrier under the table. No dripped wax from the candles, no soiled spot where the editor in chief had collapsed and died.

No doll.

Had she expected it to just be sitting around, waiting for her?

"Hey, if you can hear me, I don't want you to hurt anyone else."

Worth a try, but naïve to think it could actually work.

She would be damned lucky if it didn't backfire. It reminded her of when her mother had told her to stop reading "trash" like *The Exorcist*. Lot of good that had done.

She went into the break room to pick up Digby's pop—*Diet Rite, none of that RC crapola*—and then headed to her office. She needed to find her handbag with her compact. Her plan, if it could even be called that, was to tell Digby everything. The doll, his father's role, Agnes's suicide—everything. Cleaning herself up wasn't necessary, but looking like a bag lady who'd been dumpster-diving wasn't going to help her cause. Especially when it came time to convince Digby that there were forces beyond this world at play here.

Lussi stashed the pop inside the box and tried her office door-knob. Unlocked. Good news since her key ring was inside her handbag . . . which was right there on her desk, where she'd left it. Her coworkers might have rummaged through it but they hadn't thrown it out. That was nice of them. She pulled the chain on her desk lamp and sat down.

She fished her compact out. The light wasn't all that bright in here, but it was enough. She snapped open the compact and raised the mirror to eye level. She'd touch up her foundation, and then—

She inhaled sharply.

Someone was standing behind her.

There was only a small gap, maybe two feet, between the back of her chair and the bookshelf. Impossible for someone to be in that space and for her not to hear them, not to feel them. And yet. The figure was tall. Too tall to be human. It was veiled in darkness, the only color two bright red, burning eyes. She was gazing into the abyss through the mirror, and the abyss was gazing back.

Lussi had done her fair share of abyss gazing. Always within the safe confines of fiction. Horror took you right to the preci-pice, where you could stare into the darkness without falling in. Without losing yourself. She enjoyed that feeling, giving death the finger.

She didn't enjoy whatever this was.

She craned her head only as far as she needed to in order to see what was behind her with her own eyes. She didn't know why this was important—she didn't know what it would prove or disprove, but she did it anyway.

There was nothing there except for the doll on the shelf. Grin-ning as usual.

—*detestable*—

She was almost certain it hadn't been there when she'd sat down.

She glanced back at the figure in the mirror. A glimpse of the spirit's true shape. Its edges were undefined. Blurred.

Holy. Shitballs.

It was real.

If this wasn't a dream—if she was really in her office—then all of her beliefs about how the world worked were null and void. Lussi had crossed some invisible line between what she understood was possible and what was actually true. Her assumptions about reality now belonged to a world that no longer existed.

Keeping an eye on the shaking mirror, Lussi reached for the box. She carefully lifted the lid. The ancient hinges squeaked as she flipped it open. She removed the pop. It trembled in her hand, too. Her whole body was trembling, she realized. It wasn't fear. The chair was quaking beneath her; the floor, humming under her feet. The building was rattling, as if a train were passing through the lobby.

She would have to act fast. Swing around, grab the doll, and stuff it into the box. She snapped the compact closed; she couldn't work up the courage while seeing that . . . thing out of the corner of her eye. Just pretend it wasn't there. Because . . . it *wasn't*.

The can of Diet Rite, shaken to its bursting point, sprung a leak. A fountain of pop erupted, showering Lussi. A momentary distraction, but it was all it took for things to go south. The manuscripts stacked in the corner took to the air, shooting straight at her like they'd been fired out of the world's fastest Xerox machine. Lussi crossed her arms over her head to protect her face—she needed a papercut on her eyeball like she needed an asshole on her elbow. The pages were circling her desk, a great white cyclone. Her hair was whipping around, too—Aqua Net was no match for a supernatural twister. The slush pile meant to claim another victim.

Lussi pulled the box into her lap and pushed herself away from her desk, ramming her chair into the bookshelf. A handful of paperbacks rained down on her, plunking off her head and onto the floor like Plinko chips on *The Price Is Right*. The doll tumbled off, too, landing right in the open box. She didn't take time to question her good luck. She flipped the lid closed and held the wooden box tight to her chest and waited for the storm to die down.

The whirlwind spun its way out of her office and into the hallway. Her ears popped as the air pressure changed in the room. A few final pages flitted about, taking their time falling to the ground. She snatched the last one out of the air. *In Dog We Trust*, page 174. She balled it up and tossed it across the room. The crumpled paper bounced once and then rolled for the door, rounding the corner and chasing after the cyclone.

What the hell? Why hadn't it died down? It continued to rage in the lobby, battering the building from within. She should've known better to think she could just walk in, grab the doll, and leave.

Finally, a deathly silence fell over the building. She took a moment to gather her wits and then crept slowly down the hall, box under one arm. Digby would have to forgive her disheveled appearance.

She paused at the railing to marvel at the state of the lobby. It looked like an F5 had come through, which was about what had happened. Pens, pencils, scissors, and staplers were strewn about the lobby, mixed in amongst the manuscripts that had taken flight from Lussi's office. The needles had been shorn off the Christmas tree by the wind, leaving bare wooden dowels. The scattered tinsel gave the ruinous scene the luster of midday. The cyclone appeared to have burned itself out. Lussi prayed to a god she was putting more and more faith in lately that it had been the last gasp of the Percht. The twitching eyelid of a corpse.

In the steady calm, the disquieting stillness that only follows storms, Lussi heard a muffled cry. The door to the basement was open.

The shout came again, this time less emphatic. *Help.*

Fabien.

Lussi didn't think. She ran, taking the stairs by twos and threes. Her silver bracelets jangled as she rounded the staircase, down, down, down. It wasn't until she was at the top of the basement stairs that she hesitated.

Something about this wasn't right. What was Fabien doing here? He was supposed to be on the Upper West Side, sleeping like the dead. It smacked of a trap. The setup was perfect: there was only one way out of the basement. If the door were to be locked on her . . .

Lussi heard Fabien call out again. *Help.* This time his voice was weaker. More pained. Screw it. She didn't have time to overthink this. If it were Fabien, she needed to get to him fast. She descended into the bowels of the Blackwood Building, not even slowing when the door swung shut behind her.

She was right. It was a trap. But the bait was real nonetheless.

On the floor at the bottom of the stairs, Fabien lay in a pool of his own thickening blood.

CHAPTER THIRTY-FOUR

Lussi stripped her denim jacket off and pressed it into the sucking hole in Fabien's chest. The wound was just below his rib cage on his right side. Lussi didn't have to ask how the pain was; she could tell plainly by the grimace on his face. But at least he could grimace. She'd only seen that look one other time, when he'd read a few lines of the latest Shaun Hutson. *It's vulgar as a pot of piss*, he'd said, hurling the book off his seventh-floor hotel balcony.

Lussi placed his hands on the jacket. "Can you hold that? I'll need to leave for help in a second."

He tried to speak but only managed a hideous gurgling sound. He turned his head and spit out a thick rope of mucus. "I saw you'd left while I was napping," he said. "Thought you'd come to the office to do something stupid."

"I did do something stupid. I drugged you," she said. "You shouldn't be able to walk—"

"What do you think I gave you, horse tranquilizers? It was just a couple of 'ludes. It takes more than that to knock me out. It takes . . . well, it takes a pistol, I suppose."

"How'd you get into the building?" she asked.

"I was circling it outside, looking for your office. I suppose I was going to throw rocks at your window but I couldn't remember which one it was. Heading through the alley, I heard a loud bang. Like someone lit a firecracker up my arse. Then . . . I woke up here." He lifted the soaked denim jacket. Blood continued to pool where he'd been shot. "This doesn't look like my coat."

"You didn't see who did this?" she asked, ignoring his quip about the jacket. There were more pressing matters. "You didn't see a cloak or a mask?"

He shook his head.

She looked up at the basement door. "I'm going to go get help. Don't go anywhere."

Fabien made a gurgling noise. "Fat bloody chance of that."

She raced upstairs and jiggled the door handle. It was locked, which she'd known it would be, of course, but any hope it had swung shut on its own died. She threw her shoulder into it. No give; it wasn't as flimsy as the cage door. She banged on it with her fists, hollering for help, praying her voice would carry to Digby on the fourth floor. "How hasn't he heard a damn thing? There was a freaking tornado in the building a few minutes ago," she muttered to herself.

Lussi walked back down the stairs, defeated. Fabien was silent. He lay there, using his waning energy to hold the jacket against his body. She gently lifted his hand. "Here, let me do it. If I'm stuck down here, I might as well be of some use."

That's when she smelled it. Obsession for Men.

"Fabien," Lussi said, her voice shaking ever so slightly. "I think I know who did this." She closed her eyes and pictured Digby stepping into the alleyway and shooting Fabien point-blank. Dragging his body to the basement. The cloying scent of Fabien's cologne rubbing off on Digby's clothes.

But why shoot Fabien? It didn't make any sense.

You know the answer, Lussi, a voice whispered in the back of her mind.

As bait for me? Lussi wondered.

Think harder. There's nothing to be gained by trapping you here.

Lussi shook her head. She didn't want to believe it.

Digby knows. He's figured it out. He's making an offering to the Percht. Just like his father did before him.

He's spoiled but he's not a murderer, Lussi thought, fighting against the voice in her head.

He's been looking at the financial records for weeks now. If he knows what the Percht has to offer, and can secure his father's legacy with a little sacrifice, why wouldn't he do it? Fabien means nothing to him. You mean nothing to him.

"You warned me about this place," Lussi said, opening her eyes and looking down at Fabien. "I should have listened."

Fabien coughed hard. "It's all blood under the bridge. You need to promise me one thing, though."

"Don't you freaking dare. We're not saying goodbye. We're locked down here, but there has to be a way to signal somebody for help. A fire alarm . . . something. We'll have an ambulance here in no time—emergency services is well acquainted with the address."

He didn't respond, not right away. His breathing had slowed significantly. He wrapped his fingers around hers. "Unless I come back as a ghost, I think I'd better say what I have to say now." He coughed again. "I want you to promise me that after I'm—after . . ."

"Fabien?"

His eyes fluttered. He fixed them on her. "Promise me," he said between wet gasps, "promise me you won't let my books go out of print."

He closed his eyes. A thin smile spread on his lips.

She laughed. In spite of herself, she laughed. "That's not going to happen. Your new book . . . it's everything you said. It's so fuck-ing good. So fucking good." Her face was streaked with tears again. "You're making me cry at work, too. I don't care. Your backlist isn't going anywhere. People are going to read you for a long, long time."

He didn't respond. He hadn't even heard her; his thin smile was frozen in place. Each breath was more spaced out than the last. His hands went cold and slack. She pressed the jacket hard against his wound. If the bleeding had slowed at all, it was because there was precious little fluid left in his veins. He was fading like an ellipsis . . . and she couldn't do a damn thing about it.

Or could she?

There was one avenue she hadn't explored.

She'd finally reached the suicide part of her suicide mission.

Lussi looked at the box next to Fabien's rapidly dying body. She removed the bracelets from her wrists and tipped the box's lid back, exposing the doll.

The lights flickered and went out.

CHAPTER THIRTY-FIVE

At first, there was only darkness. Then darkness upon darkness. A shadow, a whisper. The whisper of a shadow. Lussi wasn't sure if what she was seeing had form or if the darkness was simply playing games with her. Whatever it was, it was quiet as the predawn hours of Christmas morning. It was everywhere and nowhere all at once. She tried to trail the shadow around with her eyes, but it eluded her like a floater on the edge of her vision.

"I can feel you," she whispered into the dark.

The mesh cages rattled in response. She'd felt the Percht's presence before—she recognized the electrical charge running through her from that first time in the basement—but never this strong. This naked. The electric feeling had been there in the background all along, growing, slow and steady, since she'd made first contact with Xavier Blackwood's doll—the doll that was so much like the one she'd known but not. The doll was but an anchor. The presence swirling around her was the spirit's true self. The thing in the mirror.

The thing taking form in the basement with her had no relationship to the Percht she grew up with. Oma's doll had never had power, as far as she knew. Xavier's doll was a lightning rod.

It had been charged long ago. Whether it was the result of Third Reich supernatural experimentation or pre-Christian pagan rites was beside the point. All that mattered was whether or not Lussi could control it.

There was only one way to do that, if what Agnes had said was true.

What Xavier Blackwood had done to keep the publishing company afloat all these years was unthinkable. He'd sacrificed interns to survive industry turmoil and changes. His competition had been reduced via mergers and acquisitions. Bankruptcies. His "boy" had allowed Blackwood-Patterson to weather the ups and downs of publishing. The company had never made a profit; it didn't have to. The Percht couldn't make a book a best seller, but Xavier seemed to have found a way to use it for cash influxes. His own private ATM.

But Lussi didn't want money.

Fabien's breathing was so shallow now as to be silent. She squeezed his wrist and held it tight, waiting eons until she felt a pulse. If he were conscious, he would try to talk her out of what she was about to do. He would have probably been successful, too. It was a good thing for him that he wasn't awake.

"Are you hungry?" she asked, casting her voice into the darkness.

Mein Frauchen, the thing said. *Fütter mich, mein Frauchen.*

———

Lussi had played hardball with some of the toughest agents in the industry.

This deal did not take long.

———

There was a great KER-THUNK inside the service elevator shaft. The gray doors slid open, revealing an elevator cage lit by a bank of overhead fluorescents and illuminating a kneeling figure. Alan. The maintenance man grumbled to himself as he fiddled with the control panel. An array of tools was spread out beside him.

"Um, hello?" Lussi said.

He looked up, startled. His thin white hair was a mess, making him look like a mad scientist. "Oh, you again," he said, relaxing. "What do you got there, a body? I left my handsaw upstairs. Leave him there, I'll get to him later."

"He's not dead."

"Sure looks it, though, don't he? Let me see . . ." He picked through his tools and raised a hammer. "This should do it."

Lussi put up her hands. "I don't want him dead. I need your help getting him upstairs."

"Well, why didn't you say so?" Alan said, hopping to his feet.

The maintenance man's willingness to engage in criminal activity disturbed her, but it shouldn't have. If Alan really did have ten children at home, what choice did he have? He couldn't afford to lose his job. Not in this economy. And yet he would end up on unemployment anyway when the company went under. That outcome was all but guaranteed. Even if *Transylvanian Dirt* was the game changer she believed it to be, Blackwood-Patterson's luck had run out.

CHAPTER THIRTY-SIX

The service elevator opened on the fourth floor, down the hall from the great oak doors leading into Digby Blackwood's office. The elevator wasn't as old as other parts of the building, but the ride had been harrowing nonetheless. The car had taken its time climbing the floors, the gears grinding in fits and starts. But it worked. Mighty fine coincidence that Alan had gotten it into serviceable condition the exact moment she needed it . . .

She stepped out alone. The maintenance man stayed inside the elevator with Fabien's slumped body. Alan had agreed to take him to the nearest hospital. She wasn't sure she trusted the wily maintenance man—she had come to believe he was the one who'd dropped trou in her office after all—but she had no choice.

"Go to the emergency room," she stressed one last time. "Not the morgue."

Alan nodded as the elevator door closed. Lussi would take the stairs back down, provided she was in any condition to when the time came. There were no guarantees. Even with the backing of a metaphysical entity. Otherwise, Xavier Blackwood would still be here.

She saw a sliver of light underneath the doors to Digby's office.

Lussi hadn't been up here to see him since he'd taken over. The afternoon of her interview was still the only time she'd been in the fourth-floor office, which extended the building's length from front to back, with magnificent views all around. She took a deep breath and exhaled. She raised her hand to knock.

"It's open," Digby said from within.

She pushed the doors apart. A strong sense of déjà vu struck her upon seeing him behind the desk. The resemblance to his old man was uncanny. They had the same high cheekbones, the same Roman nose. Digby's features were starting to harden. He seemed to have aged a decade in the past two weeks.

"That doesn't look like my soda," he said, staring at the wooden box in her hands.

She crossed the room and thunked it down on his desk. She didn't sit. The chair was the same too-tall chair she remembered from her interview. Digby hadn't changed any of the furniture or bothered to replace his father's things on the bookshelves. "Forgive me," she said. "It's been a long day, mostly because of the thing inside this box."

"Huh," was all he said. He cut a line of gray powder on a mirror on his desk and, using a bit of straw, snorted it. He threw his head back and yelled, "Goddamn, that's some good shit."

Digby pushed the mirror across the desk.

Lussi shook her head. "No thanks. I'm with Nancy Reagan on this one."

"It's not coke," he said. Digby dipped a finger into the small pile of powder on the mirror. He rubbed it over his gums and teeth. It gave him a ghastly appearance, like he'd been eating dirt. "It's Daddy," he said with a giggle. "It's *Daddy*."

For the first time, she noticed the open urn beside the desk lamp. His father's desk . . . his father's lamp. His father.

"You're sick," she said. "You need help."

He placed a palm on top of the box. "Is this what I think it is?"

"How would you even know what it is?"

He opened the box and stared at the doll. "My father's lawyer handed me a sealed letter at the funeral. It explained everything. I couldn't believe it at first, but the more I thought about it, the more it made sense." He looked at the doll almost wistfully. "I always wondered what was in this box. By the time I was tall enough to get it down from the shelf, I'd forgotten about it. But I never forgot how my father kept me at a distance—how he loved this company more than me. More than my mother. More than Agnes, even. He always preferred books to people. Hence this whole shambling enterprise."

"Stop," she said. "I'm beginning to like him."

He slapped the table, sending a small plume of powder into the air. "He could have used this doll to get rich. If you're going to make a deal with the devil, at least make some *bank*. This building . . . everything he worked for . . . his priorities were all backward. Now he's a pile of dust. This building will be a pile of dust in a few weeks, too."

"Let me guess . . . you're going to torch it for the insurance money."

He shook his head. "Selling it to a developer. It will go the way of every other old building in this rat-infested neighborhood. I was holding off to see if you could find me the next Stephen King, but I take it you're turning in your resignation."

"You shot the next Stephen King."

He looked up at her. His pupils were unnaturally dilated. "The fatso I caught trying to break in? He's not even American."

"Fabien is a naturalized citizen. Not that it makes any difference."

He snorted another line, then pinched his nose. "I used to be a hotshot on Wall Street. Had a run of bad luck. Went balls deep into debt to the wrong people. The plan had been to cash out, to sell my father's business when it looked like we were on an upward trajectory. Now that I have this, it doesn't really matter, does it? This is worth ten times any publishing house in this city."

Digby reached into the top desk drawer. He pulled out Gail's Desert Eagle and pointed it at Lussi, but she stood her ground. "I don't need your dumb British writer. I don't need *you* anymore."

Lussi watched as he pulled the trigger.

———

Nothing.

Not even a click.

"You've got to be shitting me," he said, peering down the barrel with one eye. He was squinting the other. "Jammed? Christ."

Lussi breathed a sigh of relief. She'd known Digby still had the gun. But she had something better: Perky. She'd struck a deal to save Fabien's life. Now she had to follow through on her end of the bargain.

Digby turned his ire on the doll, still in the box. "I left you a sacrifice. I thought that was your thing—spill some blood, show you that I'm serious. Show you that I'm worthy. What's that? You want *another* sacrifice? If you insist."

He lunged across the desk at Lussi, snagging her sweater. She drove her elbow into his forearm and he released her, screaming in pain, letting loose obscenities like, *I'm going to kill you, bitch*, and *you're dead bitch*, and *bitch bitch bitch, blah blah blah*. All the dumb things men scream at women who've wronged them.

Lussi wasn't going to stick around to listen. She bolted for the twin doors.

They were locked.

"Yoo-hoo," Digby called behind her.

She glanced over her shoulder, expecting to find him advancing on her. Instead, he was seated cross-legged on top of his desk, toying with the bowie knife. It had fallen out of her belt loop as she'd freed herself from him. He was playing with it, testing its sharpness on his palms and drawing blood like a fascinated child.

"There's a button underneath the desk," he said, without looking at her. "Locks the door remotely, so that you can't leave. Discovered it by accident. Not sure what kind of games the old man was into."

"I can guess," Lussi said.

Digby stood tall on the desk. He looked at his bleeding palms. His self-administered stigmata. "Is this enough blood, you stupid doll?" he said, hopping onto the floor. He was wobbly on his feet, but not wobbly enough to cripple him. Only enough to level the playing field between them. He pointed the bowie knife at her. He was desperate now; dangerous. Much more dangerous.

She needed to reach that button under his desk.

He grinned, showing his blackened gums again. He stalked her around the room, swinging the knife wildly. "I'm going to cut you to ribbons, and when I'm done, I'm going to string your intestines like garlands around the office. How do you like the sound of that?"

"I've heard worse pickup lines," she said, dodging a clumsy stab. All it would take is one thrust, one cut along her jugular or to an artery, and she'd never see the light of day again.

Had Perky abandoned her, too? Was Digby's bloodlust tickling its fancy?

Digby swiped at her again and she bent backward nearly to the floor. With every step back, she edged closer to the desk. All she had to do was hit that button. Then she could make a run for it.

Finally, she reached the desk. He'd backed her up to it.

He thought he had her. Silly boy.

Lussi rolled onto the desk and over it, falling into the chair. She steadied herself with her left hand on the desk to keep the chair from rolling back and felt for the button underneath with her right. *There.* She slapped it and heard the doors swing open.

But it was too late. Digby was on her, driving the knife down into her hand on the top of the desk, through her palm and into the leather-padded wood, nailing her in place. There was no pain, just pressure. Her entire left arm went stiff and numb. Dark red rivulets welled up around the edges of the blade.

"Is this enough blood for you?" Digby asked the doll. It didn't respond.

Digby rested his hand on the bowie knife. Lussi thought he meant to finish her with it. Instead, he plucked the doll from the box and walked out, leaving her pinned in place. Lussi didn't try to stop him. Digby was a bolting bank robber, unaware of the dye packs about to explode inside his sack of cash.

Lussi heard him march downstairs and out the front door.

She heard squealing tires. A dull thud.

After a few minutes, sirens.

And then everything faded to black.

CHAPTER THIRTY-SEVEN

Lussi dreamt the building was on fire. She watched it burn from the curb from across the street, alongside the gutter punks and the homeless, the protestors and the addicts. The flames were shooting high into the night sky, carrying Blackwood-Patterson into the past. History was burning right before their eyes. Every editorial letter, every first printing. Every record. Every scrap of paper; every Post-it note. She could hear the crackling and snapping as the fire it feasted its way through the building. Every floor. Every room. Every thing. No matter how much water the firemen flooded it with, they weren't going to save the Blackwood Building. All that would be left of the historic structure in a few short hours would be a charred iron skeleton. Blackwood-Patterson wasn't a phoenix capable of rising from the rubble. The intellectual property would be sold at auction, acquired by a Midtown publisher to beef up their backlist. Her coworkers would scatter. It would be Broken Angel all over again. It began to snow, and she opened her mouth to the sky, tongue out to catch the flakes. The snow wasn't pure white, but dark gray. It wasn't snow, she realized as it coated her tongue with a chalky residue. It was ash. So much ash . . .

CHAPTER THIRTY-EIGHT

Lussi sneezed, and Xavier's ashes scattered in a gray plume. She lifted her head off the mirror. So that explained the chalky taste in her mouth. She didn't know how long she'd been asleep, but Xavier's fourth-floor office was flooded with sunlight. Her lower back felt like she'd spent the night on a futon in the devil's dorm room. She was seated in the old man's tall leather chair, where she must have slept hunched over the desk. Good news, though—her left hand was no longer pinned to the desk. Someone had bandaged it.

As she slowly came to, she became aware of somebody sitting across from her. The intern. Cal, who had not died. His crutches were leaned against the desk, and he was seated in the chair that had almost swallowed her whole during her job interview. Cal was watching her with great interest, a steaming coffee in his hands.

"That had better be for me," she said.

"Black, no sugar," he said, placing her *Phantom* mug on the desk. "I was just keeping my hands warm. The front door was open when Gail got in this morning. You don't feel that? It's freezing in here."

"I feel like I'm on fire," she said. The Christmas sweater she'd borrowed from Agnes was soaked through with sweat.

"Probably your hand. Might have an infection setting in." He fished two fat burgundy pills from his shirt pocket. "Painkillers. Until you can get to a doctor. Oh, and before I forget, your friend Mr. Nightingale left a message—he's not dead."

"That's all his message said?"

Cal pulled a Post-it note from his shirt pocket, followed by his glasses. How much stuff could you keep in a polo pocket?

"Not dead," he read off the note. "Yep. That's what it says. 'Not dead.'"

Lussi swallowed the pills. The coffee was weak. Cal would need to work on that.

"Let's go down to my office," she said, rising to her feet. "Get out of here before Digby—"

"Ah, I suppose you haven't heard, what with you being pinned to the boss's desk with a knife. There was an accident," Cal said. He put some bass into his voice to indicate his seriousness. She found it adorable. "You'd better sit down for this."

━

Cal told Lussi what she already knew: at three thirty-four this morning, Digby Blackwood—heir to the Blackwood-Patterson publishing house—was hit by a checkered taxi on the sidewalk as he exited the building. The driver had been arrested on suspicion of driving while impaired. He'd blown a .235. Lussi covered her mouth, trying to project the appropriate amount of shock and horror. It was easy to fake. A blood alcohol level like that was rather impressive.

"Not another car on the road at that hour," Cal said, shaking his head. "The road conditions might have played a part. Bad luck all around."

The Blackwood family's luck would grow even worse once Agnes was discovered. Lussi had left the body where it was but washed, dried, and put away her coffee mug and fruitcake dishes before leaving. It was as if no one else had ever been there that night. She had left the front door open, hoping that it would attract the attention of neighbors. It hadn't seemed right to let the woman go undiscovered for too long.

There was a knock at the double doors. "Come in," Lussi said.

It was Sloppy Joe. He glanced at Cal and handed a paper to Lussi. It was a typed-up list of a dozen names. All Blackwood-Patterson employees. Brian. Stanley. Rachael. None of them she'd worked closely with, except for Mary Beth Wilkerson, whose name was starred.

"What am I supposed to do with this?" she said.

"It's the list," Sloppy Joe said.

"The list."

"The ones who voted to . . . you know." Sloppy Joe made a throat-slash gesture. "The ones with the asterisks are the ones who tied you down. I was there. Undercover." He lowered his voice. "I set you free."

Cal nodded. "When the meeting turned into a witch hunt the other day, I began to suspect something strange was going on around here. I knew I could trust this big fella, though. He's a fellow cinephile."

"Praise Hollywood," Lussi said.

"What do you want to do about them?" Sloppy Joe asked. His eyes flicked back to the doors. He'd left them open a crack.

"What *can* I do?" she said. "I'm not getting the police involved, if that's what you're thinking."

Sloppy Joe got an evil glint in his eye. "You could turn them into newts."

She glared at him.

"Or fire them," he said quickly.

She set the paper down on the desk next to the box. The empty box. "And how am I supposed to fire them? That was in Digby's job description, not mine."

"You're the only one here with a senior title," Sloppy Joe said.

"I'm sorry, what are you trying to tell me? That I'm . . ."

Sloppy Joe nodded. "You're the boss now, boss."

Lussi hadn't expected to vault straight to the top. She'd been prepared for more internal resistance, more political jockeying. At least that was how she'd imagined it last night when she'd made the deal. She'd offered to unshackle the Percht—to let it loose upon an unsuspecting world and free it from the iron cage of the Blackwood Building in exchange for Fabien's life. A lowball offer. A starting bid. One it rejected outright, as she'd known it would.

Worth a shot, still.

Like Xavier Blackwood, the Percht was as much a part of the building as the soot-black brownstone veener. What had Agnes called it? A "house spirit." Asking it to leave—or, worse, attempting to evict it—was futile. The best outcome she could hope for was to come to terms with it. By the time they'd metaphorically shaken hands, she had handed Digby Blackwood over on a platter. He died not understanding his ploy for the doll's affection had fallen on deaf ears.

Lussi would not allow the building to be sold to developers. She was confident she could convince whoever inherited Blackwood-Patterson from Digby to hold on to both the building and the publishing house. And if they didn't want to . . . she now had ways to make things happen.

Lussi told Sloppy Joe to let the eavesdroppers in. He swung the doors open and Brian stepped gingerly into the office, as if he were testing the temperature of a pool. Rachael followed close behind, staying far from the windows. When Dracula's Brides entered, the floodgates burst. The employees poured into the office in twos and threes, packing it from bookshelf to bookshelf. Alan was the final one to arrive, clear in the back. When he nodded to her, Lussi rose and stepped on top of a stack of her predecessor's books she had placed at her feet.

"First, let me say how sorry I am to hear about Digby," she said. "Many of you knew him from the time he was a little boy, and I can only imagine how difficult this is. Especially after what happened to his father. And what happened to Mary Beth. And Stanley. And Agnes. And—"

"What happened to Agnes?" someone shouted.

"She quit last week," Lussi said without missing a beat. "Only the second employee to ever leave this company, as I understand it. Which brings me to my next point: no one else is losing their job." Sighs of relief. "It has been brought to my attention that there was a training exercise that got out of hand last night. Some of you were there; some of you weren't. All of you had some culpability, though." Lussi bit her lip and shook her head. A twin bill of disappointment she'd picked up from her mother. "That's all in the past. We need to come together if we're going to get through this rough patch. Xavier Blackwood left some big shoes to fill, and I need every hand on deck. So let's let bygones be bygones. Besides, Christmas is just around the corner. 'Tis the season of forgiveness."

Lussi Meyer surveyed the room from behind the majestic desk where two generations of Blackwoods had presided. She was the first woman to occupy the executive office. The first non-Blackwood. Her coworkers—soon to be her employees, once the paperwork was worked out—were nodding in agreement with her. She wanted to say something powerful, something poetic. Something Dickensian, in the spirit of the season. Instead, she said, "Who's ready to publish some horror books that are going to make people shit their pants?"

It wasn't Dickens, but it brought out tears just the same.

CHAPTER THIRTY-NINE

At the end of her first full day as publisher, Lussi took a moment to enjoy the view from her new office. The sun was setting behind the building, casting a brilliant orange glow over the clouds. The park below seemed less threatening from this height, the vagrants and their problems less troubling. A few short weeks ago, she could have never conceived of an office with a window. Now she had an office with a panoramic view of the city.

And the price? Ah, the price. As Michel de Montaigne said, there was no more expensive thing than a free gift. Already, Lussi could feel the corrupting influence of the Percht in the way she viewed the park denizens. Or maybe it wasn't the doll. Maybe it was what happened when you climbed the ladder—the farther you went, the less you could see. The less you were forced to see.

As the sky darkened, the spirit's reflection sharpened in the windowpane. The doll was now sitting on the bookshelf behind her—the same bookshelf she'd accidentally knocked it from during her interview. Or not so accidentally, as she was beginning to believe. Cal had found the doll on a street vendor's blanket during lunch. He'd paid two bucks for it. Hadn't the slightest idea that it had been thrown from Digby's hands in the accident. He'd simply remembered Lussi's description of Perky from the other day when she'd asked if he'd seen it. She patted Cal on the head like a puppy and thanked him. He was earning every penny he wasn't being paid.

Lussi didn't feel the need to put the doll in its box. Not yet. She could sense the spirit's hunger was satiated. No harm in leaving it out for a few hours. Maybe a few days. Let it stretch its legs. When it started acting ornery again, though—playing pranks, breaking legs, or worse—she would need to box it up. Put its dark magic on hold.

She pulled the list from her jeans pocket. Lussi had forgiven the Blackwood-Patterson staffers who had voted to eliminate her, but she would not forget. When it came time to balance the books at the end of the year, she would need to feed the Percht again to get it to work its magic for her. It would help to have dinner ready.

EPILOGUE

"Tell me, Ms. Meyer, when was the last time a Blackwood-Patterson book hit the *New York Times* best-seller list? As a woman, I respect everything you've done—I'm not denigrating your track record. *Transylvanian Dirt* and its sequels have sold, like, a bazillion copies. I'm guessing those books kept the lights on around here through the financial crisis. Outside of Fabien Nightingale, though, horror is dead. Has been since the early nineties. You and I both know the so-called 'horror boom' was a fad. Readers got tired and moved on. Even the great Stephen King ditched the genre. He's writing mysteries now—finally decided to relinquish the crown to Nightingale, I guess.

"Walk into any bookstore today—independent, Barnes and Noble, take your pick—and look for the horror section. There isn't one. Young adult, though—that's where you can still get away with horror. Just don't call it 'horror'—they prefer the term 'paranormal.' Less scary. Oh, and you need to throw in some romance. Teens and their hormones, y'know? Everybody's heard of *Twilight,* of course. There's also *Beautiful Creatures, Vampire Academy* . . .

"Wait, you've never heard of *Vampire Academy*? O-M-G. You would love it. There's twelve books, but start with the first one.

There are two types of vampires, plus Rose, who is a dhampir—a human-vampire hybrid—and there's this boy, Dimitri—so, so hot—and the whole thing takes place at a . . .

"Yes!!! At a vampire academy. See, you're catching on. Skip the movie, though. They say the movie is always better, but not in this case . . .

"'The book is always better'? Never heard it that way. Maybe a hundred years ago or whatever. But with the advances in CGI technology . . .

"I've got the internship? Seriously? I won't let you down, Ms. Meyer. All my girlfriends said, 'Why would you want to work there? They're living in the past.' But I don't know, I think what you do here is quaint. I love the building—so, so retro. All the vintage flickering bulbs, the faux-wrought-iron brushing on everything . . . and that doll. I just loooooove that doll. So spooky! My grandmother has one just like it . . .

"Is something wrong? You don't look so well . . . Oh, God. I'm calling for an ambulance. Hang in there, Ms. Meyer . . . hang in there."

ACKNOWLEDGMENTS

Merry Christmas to everyone at Quirk Books, especially my editor, Jhanteigh Kupihea, who pitched the idea of doing a horror novel centered on a Secret Santa office gift exchange.

Happy holidays to Brett Cohen, Nicole De Jackmo, Jennifer Murphy, Moneka Hewlett, Rebecca Gyllenhaal, Jane Morley, Mary Ellen Wilson, Christina Tatulli, Kelsey Hoffman, John J. McGurk, Andie Reid, and Ryan Hayes.

Adam Rabalais—thank you for the glorious cover illustration. May your days be merry and bright.

Wishing my agents, Brandi Bowles and Mary Pender at UTA, a season full of yuletide cheer.

Season's greetings to Angel Melanson, Martin Aguilera, Clay McLeod Chapman, and Grady Hendrix for their generous support and feedback.

Glad tidings of comfort and joy to my family, whose influence can be felt throughout this book. My unapologetic love of '80s horror novels will forever be tied to memories of swapping used paperbacks with Grandma Shaffer. Special shout-outs to Aunt Patti—who took me to see *Gremlins* more times than was probably healthy—and to Grandpa Dars, who introduced me to VHS creature features such as *Critters* and *Ghoulies* over my grandmother's objections. And, of course, thank you to my parents for letting me check out whatever horrifying shit I wanted from the Fairfax Public Library.

Finally, a *joyeux Noël* to Tiffany Reisz, my first reader and second wife—all I want for Christmas is you. And a stocking filled with Peanut M&M's.